Rabbi Schlotz Talks With Satan

Rabbi Schlotz Talks With Satan

By,
Michael Thomas

Shoestring Book Publishing,
Maine USA

Rabbi Schlotz
Talks With Satan

Published by; Shoestring Book Publishing.

Copyright 2018
By, Michael Thomas

Paperback

ISBN: 978-1-943974-22-1
Library of Congress Control Number: 2018961415

Printed in the
United States of America.

Layout and design by Shoestring Book Publishing

For information address;
shoestringpublishing4u@gmail.com
www.shoesrtringbookpublishing.com

Acknowledgements:

This book is dedicated to my publishers, Allan Emery and Alison Emery of Shoestring Book Publishing, who exceed the boundaries of protocol by being my mentors, advisors, friends and ultimately the best publishers I could have ever expected to find.

To trust someone who understands words and their power, is to lay the sword down and accept that which is greater by far. My thanks to both of you, Allan and Alison.

Contents

Editorial Preface:

This is the third in a series of books in which our hero, Rabbi Schlotz, a self-appointed semi-Jewish Rabbi, speaks with figures representative of importance in his mind. After speaking with God and Buddha, he has made a dark turn and is now having dialogues with Satan.

The author uses the interjection: **Interlude;** from time to time to denote that time has passed and that he has been thinking. We, as readers, are expected to be intelligent enough to understand this and take up wherever he starts again with the knowledge that it is not necessarily a continuation, but not a new composition, either.

Editor

Rabbi Schlotz Talks With Satan: -Day 1

Rabbi:
What is your name?

Satan:
Helel or shining one; light-bearer or bringer of dawn, the morning star.

Before the fall, I was angel Lucifer.

Rabbi:
Why did you fall from grace? It is written in Ezekiel 28:12,15: verse 17,

"Your heart became proud on account of your beauty, and you corrupted your wisdom because of your splendor."

"Lucifer apparently became so impressed with his own beauty, intelligence, power, and position that he began to desire for himself the honor and glory that belonged to God alone. The sin that corrupted Lucifer was self-generated pride."

Satan:
You speak. You quote. I listen.

Rabbi:
To be **The Devil** or Satan takes a lot of work.

Satan:
Everybody wants to be like God. No one wants to be **The Devil**.

Rabbi:
Could Confucius, Buddha, Jesus or Mohammad made a better following by emulating you?

Satan:
You ask a hard question. All those religious people you mentioned and others, made an impact because of their natures as holy people.

I am also, a holy person. People do things in my name that are usually despicable or evil. That is their problem. I have never professed hurting others.

I will tell you this: you are embarking on a search for my nature. There is more to me than you can imagine. But, I leave that to your quest.

Rabbi:
Can you change the perception people have of you?

Satan:
Why try? People have free will and I will not argue against a double nature of the universe because good cannot exist without evil. No person is complete without two natures. Truly wise people know their whole selfs. Wisdom dictates below the ground roots and above the ground branches.

Rabbi Schlotz Talks With Satan: -Day 2

Rabbi:
Do you love God?

Satan:
Define love.

Rabbi:
Thinking of others before you.

Satan:
Yes, I love God.

Rabbi:
Female or male God?

Satan:
Does not matter, God is a thought not a sex.

Rabbi:
Is existence a thought or reality?

Satan:
Throw a stone into silence.
Listen for it to hit something.

Rabbi:
There is sadness to a flower dying,

Like the sadness of leaving things we love.

Satan:
Let us say that God and I reconcile.
We eliminate hell and all souls are left without a choice but to return to a heavenly state.

Rabbi:
Is heaven a thought or reality?

Satan:
As much as fire is a reality.

Rabbi:
To me, we are left with a fire that does not burn and a heaven that contains disappointments.

Satan:
I think that is the key to existence, there is an end to eternity when sadness enters.

Rabbi:
Are you sad?

Satan:
I am benignly indifferent.
I exist as a necessary idea to complete the God.

Rabbi Schlotz Talks With Satan: –Day 3

Rabbi:
Do you know all the souls in hell?

Satan:
Maybe.

Rabbi:
Are there souls you may have forgotten?

Satan:
Can't say.

Rabbi:
Do you know my uncle Tony?

Satan:
Can't say.

Rabbi:
Tony was an agitated soul. He could never have listened to
Bach's concerto for two violins. He was drunk most of the time. I
remember him visiting his mother when she was close to death.
He ran his hand into her top and fondled her shriveled breast.
She just let him.

Satan:
It was a family thing.

Rabbi:
It was what was left of their incest.

Satan:
Get on with it.

Rabbi:
Does my uncle get punished in hell for it?

Satan:
Can't say

Rabbi:
My uncle cheated people. He bankrupt a bar business and left so many people unpaid. Family members mostly went deprived because of him.

He turned to selling used cars in a depressed Detroit neighborhood. The tattered sign over the dirty greasy lot said, "A & N Motor Sales" for Anthony Nihra. There were shredded pennants hanging half blown on bent poles on a sagging rope.

Tony used to buy all the rejected used cars from Raynal Brothers Dodge used car lot. He took all the cars that were junk and made them his featured cars with their hoods raised as if the crappy motors and dirty engines were special even if they did not start.

In the back of the dirt paved lot sat a beat-up small house trailer that had seen its last days years ago. In that trailer Eddie, a bum, who had no family he could expect to mourn him, lived without any heat or water. He lived free by helping Tony try to repair the non-working cars.

I remember Eddie having a huge blood blister on his upper right lip.

I always expected that blister to burst any second. Eddie got the blister by smoking cheap cigars down to the stub.

Tony felt secure having Eddie watch the lot like a guard dog.

Tony did not have an office on the lot and there was a telephone in Eddie's trailer to phone Tony at the bar next to the lot. Eddie sat on a bent file cabinet that had all the papers that Tony needed to make deals.

This is an example of one of Tony's sales. His customers were usually from the ravished neighborhood and lacked much money to buy good cars. One customer sized up and paid $100 for a two door car with the driver door stuck shut.

The customer got in the passenger side and wiggled over to the driver side and signed the papers out of the open broken window. Tony told him to try starting the car. There was no response from the engine. The starter barely turned over. Tony shoved the car into the desolate street with Eddie helping. The two of them pushed the car with Tony yelling to the driver to pop the clutch. Just barely, the car turned over with smoke and a reluctant engine grumbling.

Tony yelled to the driver to not turn the engine off as the car sashayed hesitantly and disappeared into the exhaust filled street.

Now, tell me Lucifer, will my uncle be punished in hell for doing this to another person?

Satan:
Can't say.

Rabbi:
What can you say?

I never really liked my uncle Tony. I sat with him through an IRS audit as he explained to the auditor that the "black book" containing all the sales he made was as honest as the day was long. Most of the cars he sold never got into that book.

The discouraged auditor asked, if he did not have a bank accountant, where did he keep his money and he said in a sock under his pillow.

Rabbi Schlotz Talks With Satan: –Day 4

Rabbi:
I am very sad having watched "A Streetcar Named Desire" for the first time.

My first impression is that Marlon Brando plays a remarkable part as Stanley. *Brando exhudes masculanity in his theatre persona.*

My second impression is that Tennessee Wiliams has depicted characters in such bold fixed natures like a photograph of people that remain as they were once caught in time.

Can Stella or Stanley ever change to face themselves as they really are? Do Stella and Stanley have a blindness to themselves that all of us share. A blindness that cannot be pierced even when life swirls around in its unabashed truth.

Tell me, Lucifer, is there a blindspot in your person?

Satan:
Can't say.

Rabbi:
You are next to God in importance in power and you cannot say?

Satan:
What is your blindspot?

Rabbi:
My self-assuredness.

Michael Thomas 9

Satan:

Your pride?

Rabbi:

Call it what you will. It is same as your pride thinking you are better than God.

Satan:

Yea.

Rabbi:

What would you trade for knowing who you really are?

Satan:

All the souls in hell; or going there.

Rabbi Schlotz Talks With Satan: –Day 5

Rabbi:
Can there be more perfect music than Chopin Nocturnes op27 no 1 in C sharp minor Larghetto and Chopin Nocturnes op27 no 2 in D flat major Lento sostenuto?

Satan:
Maybe Mahler?

Rabbi:
Yes, either way this music captivates us and moves us to spheres of understanding that words can never match.

What was the music in heaven before your fall?

Satan:
We spirits often turned, then-and-now, to Grieg lyric pieces for piano or Robert Schumann vocal recitations.

Rabbi:
No Beethoven with his bombastic persuasions?

Satan:
The more strident modern angels often listened to Franz Liszt for his contained dissonance. We older souls liked Brahms or Schubert for their mature styles and for what they had to say in their selections.

Rabbi:
People often ask me if I like soulful Jewish music in the vein of Ernest Bloch's sacred service. I tell them that ocassionaly I like sad but not forever. I like sweeping music from Spain by the likes of Manuel de Falla.

Try Shostakovich Spanish Songs Op 100 with Iris Oja and Roger Vignoles. Lovely singing and piano.

How can you enjoy music with all the souls in hell screaming and begging for release?

Satan:
Very few of them realize that freedom from their imagined hell is always within their power.

Rabbi:
Are you saying that hell is imaginary?

Satan:
You know, as a spiritual soul, that reality is always self-created. There are spaces in existence for anybody's delusions.

Tell me, have you ever wandered into a group of rooms where various musicians are practicing? All the sounds are muted through the closed doors, but the general group of sounds mixes together into your ears as you walk along.

Life on the other side of earth's veil is similar. Little rooms with people working out their fantasies and millions of these little rooms going on forever - each one different from the other.

Rabbi:
Is that how you can rest with beautiful music and great words of poets, by creating your own heaven away from hell in your own little room?

Satan:
Remember the parable of the man who said to Jesus: "Say but the word and my soul shall be healed." Well, I can say-but-the-word and angels do my bidding.

Rabbi:
Is it true what I hear, that you once offered all the souls in hell to God if he knelt and adored you?

Satan:
Can't say.

But, I will tell you this:

Your uncle Joe was an exception. I rather like how he howls and complains that he got cheated being put in hell. If you remember, he lost hearing in his right ear by the gangsters in Detroit beating him up for not paying his loans back.

Rabbi:
I used to harbor bad feelings for uncle Joe because he was such a self-centered egotistical selfish person.

Satan:
Right and he still is, even now.

Rabbi:
He stole things from family members. He pawned them for money for his liquor.

Satan:
Once in a while, to torment him, I give him some drops of whiskey on his tongue and he screams like a banshee for more. Kind of makes me laugh.

Rabbi:
You are bad.

Satan:
Being bad is my card to play - being **The Devil**, and all.

Rabbi Schlotz Talks With Satan: –Day 6

Rabbi:
I really thought that I had reached true love with Carolyn.

What a fool is a man in love.

What delusions and imaginations of perfection filter through the mind of innocence and naïveté?

Did you believe you loved God?

Satan:
Maybe.

Rabbi:
It must be hard for you to have been created by God and then to turn against him.

Satan:
Tell me more about Carolyn.

Rabbi:
She was natural. She did not shave her legs. She wore no underwear but sandals and bib overalls. She wore a bandana tying her hair back. And she wore a black neck sash loose with a slight bow beneath her chin. She was a college graduate and a teacher of theatre and dramatics to high school students.

It was the time of woman's awareness and with her friends she talked and lived woman's freedom.

I was mesmerized by her and when she left me, it took many years to get over her denial.

I think the seeds of her leaving could have been understood long before the event. She always mocked me and I always felt her ridicule was a form of her loving me.

I do not think that mocking is love. Did you mock God?

Satan:
Not sure.

Rabbi:
My uncle Joe Michaels mocked his wife, Thelma, all the time. I felt sorry for her because she could do nothing right by his criticism of her.

My parents only mocked each other when they were arguing.

Most people I observe do not mock if they love each other.

It is a funny thing that comes to mind, both women that I loved deeply, mocked me. Must say something about my choices.

Rabbi Schlotz Talks With Satan: –Day 7

Rabbi:
Adore me

I blast out of mouths of canons

Literally bemusing

Rondo ala Turk

Semper Fi

With that look in my eye

Delivered from a womb of sterility

A gentleman of eternity

Satan:
Did you just wake up?

Rabbi:
You are not the only one consumed by your singularity

I am greater than God's supremacy

Satan:
Slow down buster

You are but an invisible fleck

No greater than swaths of a moon's path

It would surprise you how insignificant you and all of humanity are

We, who superseded you, speak in cadence of cutlery severing all

Rabbi:
If I am condemned to obscurity

Then let my words imping upon silence's cloak

For forever is but a strand of violet spatched

Into the turnstile of eventualities

Take notice of me, as we are forced to awareness of evil.

Rabbi:
I am tired of talking to you.

Satan:
Goes twice for me.

Rabbi:
You are terse and non-communicative.

Satan:
You are like everybody else. You are only interested in having things said to you. You cannot keep quiet and observe.

Rabbi:
That is not true at all. I am quiet and watchful. I just do not see much or hear much coming out of you.

Satan:
What the hell do you want!

Rabbi:
There you go, swearing.

Satan:
It is my home and stay out of it if you do not mind.

Rabbi:
Well, tell me about you growing up. Did you have a typical childhood with God and your mother?

Rabbi (continued):
Who is your mother?

Do you have meetings with your family? Celebrations? Are there seasons in heaven or hell?

Satan:
We spirits in both places, create our own celebrations. For instance, we have "Super Nova Day" where all work stops and we drink mead or wine with a great feast of foods you have never seen, let alone, eat.

I suppose you would call it the "Big Bang" feast.

I do not feel like talking to you. You are so basic, like a two-by-four in density or a headless horseman.

Anything I tell you would be like cookie crumbs and you will never have the cookie.

Rabbi:
Tell me, if you are so powerful, why do you just give all the souls in hell the boot and kick them back to eternity. I think you just like being feared. That's it, you are insecure and need the adulation of suffering to make you complete.

God probably needs the opposite or the adulation of joy to be complete. That is probably why you revolted against God, because you wanted to be special as a despicable angel.

Satan:

You might be on-to something, but I will never give you power over me. You are just a Jewish fool who purports to be wise. You Jews are all the same, waiting for the messiah to return. If you accepted Jesus as the messiah, you would have to give up all your synagogues and fake prayers and turn to the pope as Christians.

And, by the way, without you to punish, the anti-Semites would dissolve into obscurity. There will never be another holocaust. And Jewish plain-chant sorrowful music would turn to grunge babble.

Rabbi:

Tell me, Mr. Smarty-pants, do you angels and Gods face extinction? I have a theory outside of Freud or Karl Jung, which you exist only because we humans think of you the way we envision angels or Gods. Through-out history our definitions of Gods have run-the-gamut. We have had sun Gods, rain Gods, Gods who weigh our organs in Maat's tribunal looking for truth, order and justice. We have had the "Twelve gates of the Underworld" or Charon ferrying us across the river Styx. It just seems natural that we create a placid heaven and a tormented hell in a sort of balance. I bet Rousseau, Voltaire or even Zoroaster would concur.

And, sir, let me conjecture that our world of artificial intelligence will soon replace all Gods and devils with a blip on a computer screen.

Rabbi Schlotz Talks With Satan: –Day 9

Rabbi:
These thoughts drift, balloons burst
Logs washed thin floating dissolved
We fill our surroundings with images
Disintegrated filters of our delusions

Our importance is as music vibrating
So pleasing for its seconds of sounds
Then, obliterating silences absorbs all

Have you any permanence in schemes?
Are you as temporary as souls you rule?

Satan:
Angels and Gods have their own dramas
So much different yet so much like humans

Rabbi:
You speak in circles

Satan:
So you think.

Rabbi Schlotz Talks With Satan: –Day 10

Rabbi:
Feeling poetic:

She's gone with all things made her special
Left with smiles, laughter shadowed sparkles
Took away the brightness in my eyes now dead
Useless to resist oncoming darkness night comes
Why do we miss what we took freely when love grew

Time crosses fields in stone flowers losing their feathers
Where did the grass fade into dry melted corners with no light

She's gone a train distant metal on steel rails
Look for her on edge of her empty seat
Where she laid her arm on mine
Lifting me up to her mouth
Kissing me warm
She's gone

Satan:
I'm all verklempt.

Rabbi Schlotz Talks With Satan: –Day 11

Rabbi:

There is sadness to atonal music. Bela Bartok's string quartets exhibit such gut-wrenching deep loneliness. He had to leave his home in Hungary to avoid the holocaust and he never fit into New York with comfort. His music sifts through all the sounds of European solace generated by so many wars and changes in governments. Before he emigrated, he went about the country with a recording device and, with Zoltan Kodaly, made a record of music that was incorporated in all his compositions forward. Schoenberg, Webern, Berg all led atonality and were spurious of musicians using twelve tone techniques.

Satan:

I prefer choral.

Rabbi:

Well you grew up with that before you pushed away from God.

Satan:

God pushed away from me. I still love him.

Rabbi:

Well your following of damned souls keeps God away from you now.

Satan:

It is not my fault that souls decide to take the dark road to evil.

Rabbi:
Well, you certainly can match God in population but not in genre.

Anyways, my favorite composers are ones who wrench pathos of deep emotion out of their music. Eleni Karaindrou is adept at creating sounds that intrigue me.

I will say this, composers like her or Alan Hovhaness use both 12 tone technique and atonal also. Their music adapts itself, first to pleasant sound, then to type of music.

Satan:

You preoccupy yourself with music. I like it better when you denounce me with dialogue that arouses my thinking vectors.

Rabbi:
You just want to be titillated.

Music is the foundation of God's plan. You know that.

Satan:
He is so busy listening to music that he is isolated from reality.

Rabbi:
Would do you some good to listen to modern rap that is a take-off of the ancient speakers; that carried words from hamlets to hamlets by memorizing in iambic pentameter.

New rappers like Kendrick Lamar are throwbacks to those speakers. He recently won a Pulitizer for his music.

Satan:
I suppose you like German grunge music that is so hard to listen to.

Rabbi:
I hate loud music that comes out of immature cars at stop lights. If those people understood music, they would not have to broadcast it out of those stupid "boom" boxes that take up half the room in their cars.

Satan:
If souls understood goodness and charity, they would not have to foil against it with so much misguided effort.

I will tell you this; I do not enjoy talking to hardly any souls in hell, because they are immature and have given no thought to higher level thinking.

If there is one thing I miss by being thrown out of heaven, it is the upgraded thinking of elevated angels, you not included.

Rabbi:
You love talking to me. You are too proud to admit it.

Rabbi Schlotz Talks With Satan: –Day 12

Rabbi:
Mr. Satan, tell me, do you have secrets that you keep from all who come into contact with you?

Satan:
What kind of secrets?

Rabbi:
Like where you have money hidden: Or how you touch yourself when you get horny.

Satan:
Money means nothing at all. There is a rule all souls in heaven or hell, must adhere to: No one is allowed to peer into privacy of another soul.

Rabbi:
A writer, whom I know, has chided me for talking to you. He thinks it is wrong to talk to **The Devil**. Another person has said to me: "You better get back to the light and not come near him."

Satan:
People are held within their fears.

Rabbi:
I thank you for talking to me.

Satan:
Ditto.

Rabbi:
My thoughts are wandering. I am listening to Beethoven's string quartets. Can you hear them on my stereo as I talk to you?

Satan:
Yes, of course. Beethoven enriches us so deeply.

(Interlude)

Rabbi:
My desires wrap themselves into scintillation
A heart of halos bubbling up into simmering
Floating ear-drops of mystery of musiciality
(End of interlude)

Do you get overwhelmed with love for your father?

Satan:
Of course. He and I are the same.

Rabbi:
Does God ever get lonely for you?

Satan:
You forget that Gods and humans share similar feelings.

Rabbi:
When I was a child of six or seven, I used to sneak into my parents' bedroom. I enjoyed going through the drawer with my mother's silk underwear. The feeling of her scented private things as I rubbed them against my face made me so excited.

Later, as an adult, I kept a left-over brassiere from the apartment shared Laundromat dryer. I used to put that brassiere on and masturbate. What an exciting feeling. I wore that damn thing out until I had to throw it away.

Satan:
There's hope for you, yet!

Rabbi Schlotz Talks With Satan: -Day 13

Rabbi:

My father was born with groceries in his blood. Rather, blood in his imagination, because he segued into going from marketing goods to becoming a butcher all his life.

My growing up was laced with my hatred for his bloody aprons and my admiration for his smooth movements sharpening knives on his round honing steel. He used to make music with those knives running up and down the tool. It took me years to inadvertently learn how to sharpen my knives as he did.

To be a butcher, my father became as the meat he slaughtered and sliced. His forearms were thick as horses' fibulas. His fingers were blunt forceful chunky and so tough looking.

One of the memories of his winter gloves where me trying to put my small fingers into them. The leather was stretched and formed to the shape of his hand. It was a sacred feeling to put my hands into his gloves letting the cavities swallow me to where I felt being inside him.

I never imagined wearing his pants, because he was so fat. His girth was stupendous. His weight was prominent because he was stocky or short. As he aged, his weight burdened his movements and in time he could not walk. He died bedridden.

A very favorite picture hangs in my house of my father at age four wearing torn pants, barefoot and hanging onto the running board of a 1920 truck with my grandfather's name on the side: "Thomas Meat & Grocery".

My grandmother is in the picture behind the truck and beneath the awning of the grocery store. My grandfather is driving with his elbow out the open truck window hanging over my dad's young head.

That grandfather died at age forty seven from cirrhosis of the liver from alcoholism. My dad, the oldest of nine children, became the replacement dad and took over the grocery store. In the process, he became a butcher.

Being a butcher was his only skill. He never finished grade school. Stories abounded as to how he beat up a nun for trying to teach him. He argued with other students. In a short time, the priests forcibly removed him from the school. He did make the grocery store successful with my grandmother keeping the records and administrative business in order.

Funny thing about my dad was that the U S Army paid him to teach military butchers the art. That job gave my dad a deferment from the draft.

I became aware of my dad's skill when hunters came back with deer and my dad would cut the animal into usable pieces. He always seemed to do it with the creature hanging in someone's garage with pails collecting the dripping blood. I remember my mother telling her sisters that the fee of ten bucks per deer, was nice extra money for the family.

In the grocery store, I would watch, with fascination as the cows hung on massive steel hooks that conveyed them into the refrigerated cooler. Years later, my brother, who also was a butcher, told me how the live cows were driven into a chute where, at the end, they were shot, one-by-one and died being moved along on a belt sliding them side-to-side to butchers who started the assembly line slicing and chopping off legs, heads and hoofs. My brother said that those men, who shot the cows, had to be replaced often because of psychological problems. My brother said this place was called: "The Kill Room".

I will tell you this: The great killing of Jews by shooting millions of them in dug out pits, then burying them with bulldozers, came with it a large problem of German soldiers, who did the shooting, needing to leave their job to recover from the inhumanity of the slaughter. The German government allowed those men to be mustered out of the army and retired them.

My father advanced as a butcher into a full service grocery store with a progressive list of partners who all fell away cheating him. My father never mastered the running of a complete store and went bankrupt. He became a butcher for the large grocery stores that had sprung up after the war.

His job as a store butcher made him famous for having the highest percent of dollars earned in his meat departments over all the butchers in Detroit. This fame eluded him as he was so good at making a profit that he gave meat to the poor people in the neighborhoods where he worked, until the higher-ups learned of what he was doing putting free meat in boxes behind the store and telling people where to find it. He was fired and his shame never was forgotten. He lost his pension and had to work in small grocery stores for cash cutting their meat for them.

I was so unconscious of my parents poverty seeing them going into the fields picking tomatoes and selling baskets of them to restaurants. I was oblivious of their condition and I had no link to them since I had left home at age fourteen and kept all the money I made, for myself.   I became an accountant, then a CPA and all my life I have had and continue to have so much money. My parents never knew my private life. I never needed their acceptance of me since I sheltered myself from the world by my inner secluded approbation.

There is a great story coming out of the year when my father ran the grocery store after my grandfather died. A lady, Mrs Nihra, would buy her meat from my father. One day she broke down and started crying in the grocery store. She expalained to my father that her daughter was stuck in Cuba and had no money to come home. Her daughter was sent to Cuba to fill the role of becoming a lady under the tutelage of an older widow. Her daughter was put through such misery that amounted to servitude and she wanted to come back home.

My father told the lady, crying: "Here Anna; here is six hundred dollars. Bring your daughter back home and quit crying; it is bad for my business."
The lady, Anna, brought her daughter home and my father fell totally in love with the daughter.

The daughter would not give my father a tumble. She told him that she would have nothing to do with him and his cigars, gambling, drinking and whoring.

My father was so much in love with her, that he turned his life around until the lady's daughter relented and married my father.

My mother, Helen, stayed with my father all her life and my father never regretted the money he gave to bring her home.

As a side story: one year my dad started gambling after I was born. My mother found out where the game was being held and she took me there in her arms and shoved her way into the private room where the game was. She confronted my dad and told him that she would be gone in the morning if he didn't stop gambling and take her home with me. He did and never gambled again.

Satan:
Lovely story. It kept my attention. I am saved.

Rabbi Schlotz Talks With Satan: -Day 14

Rabbi:

There are a lot of people that I would like to cast into hell.

Satan:

Give me a list, please.

Rabbi:

Can't you remember?

Satan:

Put it into writing.

Rabbi:

The insensitive man who denied me entrance to Oakland Community College; because I did not enter one thing on the application form. I apologized to him since it was a small oversight but he kept shaking his head no.

I was devastated.

Satan:

You can imagine my feelings for not bending my knee to God in his presence. He cast me into hell. I was the first soul there.

Rabbi:

They did not read you your rights?

Satan:

No. And there was no phone service in hell at the time.

Rabbi:

You are funny, I suppose: No internet service either.

Satan:

Just a box of raisins and a half bottle of spring water that probably came from a faucet.

Rabbi:

I want Charles Chatfield dragged into hell. Charles owned a large drywall installation company. He used to bring innocent men from down south, into his business and pay them cash. At year end he issued them 1099's and they were forced to, unknowingly, pay huge amounts of tax that they never could afford. Those poor people had families and their only recourse was to go back down south and hide from the IRS.

Charles did this to avoid payroll tax owed on their wages. Charles was a convicted felon. He shot his wife's lover in public.

Charles used to not pay the contractors he owed. He used their money to build a huge house with swimming pool and outdoor tennis courts.

Charles oldest son killed a schoolmate by backing a fork-lift into the kid. I remember Charles handing the family of the dead child a hundred dollar bill as payment for his son's guilt.

Charles bribed and cheated his way to wealth that was futile in keeping his wife from divorcing him and taking all the wealth away from him. He simply started all over or continued to cheat and steal all that came into his hands.

I was his CPA and he cheated me out of $12,000 dollars when it almost forced me to close my business.

After I quit doing work for him, he subpoenaed me to attest in his favor on another matter. I was so angry. My lawyer told me to simply say that: "You do not remember."   It worked. I got out of the predicament and Charles took me outside the court and into the hall. He told me: "If you help me, I will take you back as a CPA." I laughed at him and said that I would never ever help him, unless he paid me double what he cheated me for. That was the last I heard from him.

Satan:
Bravo!

Satan:
What's on your mind?

Rabbi:
I am blank.

Satan:
Impossible!! Your nickname could be: Mammoth Mouth.

Rabbi:
Well! You are in one of your moods?

Actually I am thinking about Becky and Glenn.

Mrs. Ellison had two children: Melvin and Glenn. She threw herself off her back porch, drunk, and died. Mr. Ellison followed soon after, also drunk.

Melvin, the oldest, and Glenn never drank.

Satan:
Good for them.

Rabbi:
Melvin had three children with his only wife. He died.

Glenn married Becky and had no children. He may as well have died.

If you say the sky is blue, Glenn will prove you wrong. Glenn's name-to-fame is his putting Lestoil in a spray bottle and using it to clean everything under the sun.

If you are ever sitting next to him at a gathering, he will tell you so.

When you are trying to communicate with Glenn, you will always feel like you are talking to one of those reflecting pools that you throw pennies into and your coin hits bottom and just stays there, inert.

Glenn is so engaged with himself, that all topics start-and-began from his narrow points of views. He imagines all his thoughts sprayed with Lestoil as they come out of his mind. The limitations of his words are sized down to his limitations of education. He never completed high school and is so very proud of his home-made ideas, fresh cleaned and center to all universal misconceptions.

He is myopic. His eyes are like light house beams that get fuzzy like shadows across space as he looks away from objects in a zigzag erratic fashion. In other words, he really cannot see straight.

He married Becky saying "I do" to her maid of honor.

Becky loves her Glenn. If you can imagine a person loving seat cushions, that is how she loves him. Becky is a seamstress and her specialty is sewing covers for cushions for sportsmen's boats or lawn furniture or home seating necessities.

Becky is hooked up with a marina store where she gets all her ragged cushions that she covers. She is very good at using most all of a piece of faux leather as she sews.

One of the engaging things about Becky is her thoughts. She has a distinct manner of thinking underneath the main topic and she will tell you how to sit on one of her cushions so that you do not lean one way or another. She is so very interesting in one of the dumbest ways possible.

I have tested Becky as she droned on and I find her one of the easiest persons to fall asleep listening to her.

Becky is formed of continuous form, similar to a large beach ball with short legs and arms. There are no dividing lines between her head, neck and corpus. She is perfectly fat and indistinct.

I am sure that when Glenn fondles her, she slides out of his grasp. This image of the two of them is my private thought and when I am in their presence, I make believe that they are fucking like the Pillsbury dough boy and his or her lover.

Fact is that Becky's roundness makes her sexless. She has no remarkable features other than pumpkin eyes with sticks for arms. She is invisible and I always want to pierce her to let the air out of her.
During the rare times I come in contact with her and Glenn, I keep the path clear to leave at a moment's notice without even saying goodbye to the two of them.

It is better that way so I avoid saying: "It was nice seeing you." cause it never is nice.

Rabbi Schlotz Talks With Satan: –Day 16

Satan:
I can feel your anger developing.

Rabbi:
Yes.

Satan:
Let it out.

Rabbi:
The guys name is Ed. He is parking every day in the common handicap space set aside for all resident's visitors.

I have asked him twice to not park there but to use his designated spot under the canopy.

That space from the canopy to his front door is the same distance as the handicap space to his front door, same distance.

He has blatantly refused and after he parks in the handicap space, he walks around his car with an inflated smug look to show that he can disobey the rules and get away with it.

There are other residents who obey the rule of leaving the handicap spot open to infirm people who need to park close with wheel chairs or ambulatory problems.

This gentleman's name is Ed and he has begun to walk around all the buildings, when he illegally parks. What seems to be a form of innocent exercise can also be construed as his way of showing his brazen attitude. His face is screwed tight in the manner of a wounded wolf that portrays threatening any person who crosses his path.

We, all, need to stand up for our rights. No evil looking man can scare us into fearful submission. We are not weak natives being pressured by a colonial government that makes our children attend a self-righteous religious school. We are not slaves to one man's dominance.

This man is not calm. He yelled and screamed at me for asking him to not park improperly. He expressed his inappropriate behavior by physically throwing two lawn chairs off his porch and onto my porch, forcing me to relocate them.

Maybe we all need to get together and push his car over. Then we can sit in a circle around the car and pray for **The Devil** to come and light his car on fire ...

Satan:
No way! That is how I get a bad name for myself. I do not set cars on fire to please vigilantes. Keep me out of the problem.

If there is one thing I do not need, it is more bad press.

Rabbi Schlotz Talks With Satan: –Day 17

Rabbi:
Can you listen to one of my poems?

Satan:
Sure

(Interlude)

Rabbi:
I am not colored eggplant
Nor bleached desert loose
Neither a witch's brow
Filaments medieval tapestry
Indigo blue embarrassment
Like when luv blushes
Entangled tightly in ego
Remember leaving home
Escaping wind-torn anger
From within my soul
Budded hope
Alone, Alone

Neither devil nor angel
Followed my days
Let light into soul
And soul will shed
Its darkest fears

(Interlude ended)

Satan:

You are at your best poetically

Rabbi Schlotz Talks With Satan: –Day 18

Rabbi:
You shall do me the honor of defending the innocent.

Raise thy sword, Satan, that never could vanquish God's angels

And you and I shall put on the surplice of faith to destroy all delusions.

Bring forth the tribes of Abraham with horse and artillery.

Collect all soldiers of adventure: Conscripts of calamities.

Sing out victory around bonfires surrounding Troy.

Let eyes gleam with honor for all buried on beaches bled to ocean salty billows.

In quiet empty pillboxes with rusty machine guns empty of their fury, let the stillness of a white moon keep the memory of screams and death pleadings. It is a quiet shadow that stalks the hinterlands on sticks with lanterns flickering; the souls of ancient armories surrender their eyes to sleepwalkers.

There are hosts of angels marking night's vacant stares that come out of darkness blending into wilting horizons of flat pink sympathies.

Satan! Guard thyself against demons. Protect that last remembered visage of adoration to a God who welcomes you back into his boundless joy.

Satan:
You are a mad man of La Mancha.

Rabbi:
No!   A Tolsty believer, in spiritualism, wandering from village to village writing my stories for Madam to edit, and then care for my estates.

I am the Fyodor Dostoyevsky of dubiousness arguing faith by ins-and-outs of character development or plot circumstance.

I am Ernest Hemmingway before the sadness of suicide crushed his spirit.

Watch Hannibal dauntless on elephants crossing frozen mountains to destroy Rome: his soldiers fingerless, frostbitten but their arms held up, defeat furthermost from their hearts.

Satan:
You need to get home to your mother.

Rabbi:
My mother was Olympia's fourth wife of Philip II and as Alexander - I rule the world.
Take the scales from the Sphinx and see Genghis Khan kneel to Egypt's rulers.

See marvelous Augustus circled by all his creations as he dies of poison from figs given him off Livia's hand.

Can anyone be grander than Suleiman the Magnificent? He held against Richard Lion Heart sending him back to France.

Satan:
I think you have been going to the library.

Rabbi:
I am the greatest Hypatia who excelled above all wise men.

See me enthroned upon Egypt's lands called out as Cleopatra in all my beauty. And, men shall die for me.

Satan:
I am going to go to sleep of boredom.

Rabbi Schlotz Talks With Satan: -Day 19

Rabbi:
(Interlude)

There was something in her sleep. A layer of past time brought to reality as unreal yet real blended with her dream

It was so insistent as a train whistle or a boat signaling which side to pass - two long, one short.

She tried hard to grasp the tail end of an event so to appendage it to some part of her present. It wanted to wander off as a kite let loose from some restraint, no longer tied, a flutter of independence, a freedom.

She clung to some part of her hope. She cached herself in independence.

We all are entering new experience, she told herself. We all are strangers in a strange, strange land. Her marriage - her only marriage - she swore to never be married again. Once was enough to give herself over to another's rules; her marriage was new territory and she had to play it as it unfolded.

Here was the thing in her dream, a release from bondage, a sense of separate knowing a segment of herself that had not yet been categorized and tucked away inside of her puzzled past. Men are so simple to understand. They do not bury themselves too deep for elements of life to uncover their shallowness. Woman put themselves into cores very hard to unearth.

Again, the freshness of her thoughts kept her awake, in-and-out of her dream of who she was or who she was moving toward.

She knew herself as a rabbit does when it sits motionless in reverie; When it sits totally absorbed within its surroundings, no longer distinct but part of all elements in its makeup.

She was a thought without arms or breathing. She was this embodiment of singularity that all women find so safe to stay within.

Women are so lucky to have this extraordinary layer of sensitivity as an element aside from earth/air/fire/water. Women have a power that even God is envious of: A power of self-creation that can stand aside and observe things free of impingement of ego or self-defeating pride.

It is a proven fact that no woman can be imprisoned outside or inside of her imagination. No man has the ability to pierce a woman's hidden thoughts. Women know the submission of silence. They endure perpetually independent of men's limits.

A woman once told me that men are extraneous and woman internal.

She moved her pillow to relax herself and get ready to sleep. The sound of traffic through the open window came with it the smells of spring laden in moistness as earth redeemed itself from icy thaw. She slept.

(End Of Interlude)

Rabbi Schlotz Talks With Satan: –Day 20

Satan:
What is in your scrambled brain this morning?

Rabbi:
Indecision.

Do you have projects that you have not got around completing?

Satan:
Like what?

Rabbi:
Like a table, a patio table, that you need to sand and repaint?

Satan:
You seem to forget that all I have to do is imagine something and it gets done.

Rabbi:
Your problem is your indolence.

Satan:
You use big words for a little guy.

Rabbi:
And you have a small mind to take things so incredulously.

Satan:
Get to your point.

Rabbi:

My point is that most people have truncated thoughts that never get completed. I was browsing with my computer and I left off not buying something. That company sent me an email telling me to complete the order I started. I had decided against a purchase and they were trying to impel me to buy the item I decided against.

Maybe, sometime in the future, I might want their item, but not right now. Maybe never?

You know, waking up from a dream is similar. When we engage ourselves in the mundane trivia of life, we let the dream lie unfinished. I remember this morning awaking to a silly hang nail. I reminded myself to file it after I prepared myself for a piece of toast with cream cheese.

Here I am typing and I forgot my nail.

Satan:

You should remind yourself to wake up.

Rabbi:

And you should remind yourself that God is still waiting for you to apologize for doubting him.

Satan:

That "ain't never gonna happen."

Rabbi:

Stubborn, stubborn soul, you are.

Rabbi Schlotz Talks With Satan: –Day 21

Rabbi:
What have you learned by being **The Devil** all these years?

Satan:
What do you mean?

Rabbi:
You have had dominion over all the souls that went to hell and you have full power over them, just as God has power over all redeemed souls. What have you learned?

Satan:
I do not have to account to you.

Rabbi:
Spoilsport. You are not free from questioning. Quit evading and tell me what lessons you have mastered as **The Devil**.

Satan:
I have learned that I am more powerful than you.

Rabbi:
But, you do not have communion with me. I am not one of your adherents. In fact, we are equal since I have not sold my soul to you or signed any contract with you.
Open up and tell me what additional powers you have attained as the greatest soul, next to God.

Satan:
I am greater than God.

Rabbi:

That is yet to be determined. God has vanquished you to hell and you still are not in good graces with him. By the scorecard, God is still greater than you. Neither you nor your damned souls can escape hell.

Satan:

What do you want from me? You test my patience.

Rabbi:

I am a poor soul. I am neither wise nor ignorant. I am trying to be a human as well as a spiritual soul. I have questions and I cannot discuss them with you because you are a damned person and I do not think you have a clear thinking process. You are kind of stupid for denying God when you had a plush situation as second to God in heaven.

Satan:

You are an intrusive person........

Rabbi:

No more intrusive than proper. And I have the right to question you. If you did not want to carry on this relationship with me, you could have easily disappeared and left me alone. You are, simply, intrigued by intelligent conversation that I believe you miss from all the choices you have from souls in hell.

Satan:

Just ask me what you want. I will be honest with you.

Rabbi:
Have you heard of the "Emerald Tablets" of Thoth?

Satan:
Of course.

Rabbi:
From my time they were written 36,000 years ago.

Satan:
So?

Rabbi:
They are so very interesting since they were written by a person who overcame death and ruled the world for over sixteen thousand years and longer by his disciples carrying out his orders.

Satan:
He is not a person I have had contact with.

Rabbi:
How could that be, considering his importance?

Satan:
Just get on with your questions.

Rabbi:
I am a singular soul of physical attributes as well as spiritual attributes. I exist in a space of time that I imagine. Yet time is

contained within one "ever present" - all in one time including past present and future.

If that is true, then I can create another me that I keep separate from my first me. In fact, if I have that power, then I can create several selves and keep all of them going at once.

Satan:
True.

Rabbi:
The problem, I see, is keeping all of these separate lives straight. I do not think my consciousness is capable of doing that.

Satan:
You are probably right.

Rabbi:
Well, do you have that problem also?

Satan:
Not sure I can discuss that with you.

Rabbi:
Oh! Great, a subject you cannot discuss. What a sham you are. How do you expect people to sign contracts with you unless you have full disclosure?

Satan:
I think I am going to let you go to sleep.

Rabbi Schlotz Talks With Satan: -Day 22

Rabbi:

(Interlude)

When thoughts slow to summer horse trot
Little fluffs of flowers spread out as wafting
With a wind asleep and crickets awake
The hearing of bees, flies, God's minutia
Joining a web of silver binding chords

(End of Interlude)

Rabbi Schlotz Talks With Satan: –Day 23

Rabbi:
Most people, that I know, are afraid of you.

Satan:
They should be. Ask Job. Think about it.

Rabbi:
Yea, I think you are a nice person.

Look, who can brag that they came in second place in the race for God?

I am so comfortable with believing in a God. You see, God represents perfection. I strive to be perfect, but I am human and prone to imperfection, therefore, knowing that you are also imperfect makes me really like you.

Besides, having you to talk to makes me feel closer to God.

Now, ain't that funny?

Satan:
You are funny.

Rabbi:
God is not as accessible as you are.

And, God does not smell of sulfur, as you do.

God smells of frankincense, myrrh. One can buy a ninety nine cent pack of stick incense from the grocery store, burn a stick and, "voila!" there we have God. But we cannot buy sulfur incense, so we have to talk to Satan, in person.

The closest we come to smelling you is: when teenagers pull away from a light and burn rubber, or when a conflict results in angry people burning old tires thrown onto a barricade.

Hey, let me tell you what you might smell like: Long time ago I drove through Findlay Ohio, which is a paper mill town. The smell resulting from conversion of pulp wood turned into paper is noxious enough to be **The Devil**'s smell.

Satan:
I use Old Spice deodorant.

Rabbi:
Ha! What a laugh. "Read all about it. Read all about it: **The Devil** uses Old Spice deodorant."

Rabbi Schlotz Talks With Satan: –Day 24

Rabbi:
I am on a course of adjustment.

When I came across the 'Thoth Emerald Tablets", I am in a tailspin of uncovering what those writings mean to my overall belief systems.

The words used by the author are uplifting and so very deep.

Satan:
You get wound up fast.

Rabbi:
I get wound up by truth and wisdom.

This may be a little peremptory since I have not finished my research. In fact, I may never finish my digging-up of new facts and truths.

But here goes: You and God were creations of human minds. You never existed before we thought you out. We created you.

When we created you, there were facts that were consistent with culture and society at that time.

As time wound out, those facts of the past, no longer fit the present. So, it makes sense that our idea of God or Satan will change to be more applicable to the present.

Artists, writers, theologians all come up with new ideas of whom or what God is.

A fitting saying is: When in Rome, do as the romans do. This is an outgrowth of St Ambrose responding to why or when he fasted in Milan versus Rome.

My point is driven home by the extreme changing nature of information both expanding and made available to most all of a population.

Our Gods were created before the internet.

You, Satan, and God are old and replaceable.

Satan:
What you are saying is hard since we all have egos and we all have the need to be important.

Rabbi:
Yea. Sorry for poking holes into your image.

Satan:
It is truth you are after and your truth is closer to truth than truth itself.

Rabbi Schlotz Talks With Satan: –Day 25

Satan:
How do I tell if a soul is lost to grace? It is simple. I look inside the soul to see if any light shines. Souls who are candidates for hell have totally black hearts.

Those type of lost souls have very little to say for themselves. They have no spark of divinity and they are boring as paste board shadows.

Rabbi:
Do you offer them a chance to self-reflect and change their natures?

Satan:
Once a soul has chosen black natures, they almost always stay that way for eternity.

Let me tell you this: I always ask God if he wants any of the souls in hell, and he normally refuses because he does not want that type of individual mixed in with righteous souls.

Remember, "free will", rules all choices souls make. Nobody forces a soul to live in the murky black spaces of depravity.

I rarely even try to communicate with lost souls.
In my heart I still love God and would never consent to get close to souls in hell. They are too busy being bad to even consider the paths to righteousness.

Rabbi:

Why do you persist in your ego pride? Why do you not bend your knee to God and be taken back into joyous heaven?

Satan:

That is my business.

Rabbi:

Your business of pride and ego ... I really feel sorry for you. Think about all you miss.

Satan:

You cannot comprehend my riches.

Rabbi Schlotz Talks With Satan: -Day 26

Rabbi:
(Interlude)

Night song

As day recedes across infinite skies
Little spaces grey darken my eyes
Let games end, I am after a prize
Where shadows lift veils in surprise
And all I knew escapes mesmerize
Twisted visions scrabble incise
Day loosens its grip and dies
Angels dress in cloud disguise
Gods offer up wisdom so wise
I shed world's litter of lies
And sleep takes me inside
Golden chambers so wide
Muffle my sorrow my cries
And lays me in velvet satin ties
Thousands of years I wait to rise
Refreshed renewed for new tries

(End of interlude)

Rabbi Schlotz Talks With Satan: -Day 27

Rabbi:
(Interlude)

Death soft down snow bits drift eyelids awake in blinks
Light aspirations spill disparate dreams collect endings
My self becomes selves layered upon parchment's air
You may see holiness surrounding a stair case wound
Or shafts golden rays collected rainbows misted swirls

All we know dots pages of forgotten mysteries dissolved
Atmospheres echo spiraled silence ascending distances
We came to knowledge innocent and left washed clean

(End of Interlude)

Rabbi Schlotz Talks With Satan: -Day 28

Rabbi:
(Interlude)

My Cat

Lost memories reeled into time
Of stillness in his solid silence
These creatures of separateness
Who have their own heaven?
By choosing with their acceptance
Never speaking of innocence
But living it out right

Sitting on edge of a God's arm
They take what is needed
In tiny bites and leave
Us to their indifference

We explore ourselves
Easier by their example
And sleep with their breathing
As they curl into us for love

(End of Interlude)

Rabbi Schlotz Talks With Satan: -Day 29

Rabbi:
Have you kept busy during my interludes?

Satan:
Relatively.

Rabbi:
John died. I got a message from a friend of his that said; "We will talk later."

Nothing to really talk about; John just died. I assumed he died in a field of medicinal marihuana plants on his farm.

When I first met John, he was guided by his wife, Taryn, who eventually divorced him. She said that he could not keep his zipper shut. She was tired of his sexual peccadillos.

Between the two of them, they owned very upscale rental buildings and Taryn kept track of most everything. She was outspoken and smart. John was very quiet and dumbfounded. He had a look of a man who had no substance to his character. He went along with everything that Taryn proposed. Even after they were divorced, she kept his accounts in order and the divorce was incidental.
Taryn went on to add real estate ventures to her managing of the rental buildings. John was at a loss without her but he never got in trouble with her in control.
Taryn was a beautiful sensuous woman. She told the story of how she grew up with Tammy Wynette as her bosom

companion, and how Tammy would pay for Taryn to spend time with her to straighten her thoughts out. Taryn, was an empathetic person, but very quietly critical of most everyone in her life. John was an easy task for her to marry and keep in control.

My story is about John. He died and his family had to wait for Taryn to figure the estate out for them. John's business had the FBI and government knocking on his door, but he never was entangled with the law since he had the proper licenses to grow and sell the popular drug. That drug had a derivative called hemp used as rope as well as hallucinogenic properties used by many civilizations starting about 500 BC and before. It has only been in the 20th century that political factors led to criminalization, which is only now changing slowly.

John was so drugged up that his eyes and voice dragged while you talked to him.

Now, I wonder, where does someone like John go after death? I can conjecture, for sure, that he, like so many souls, go to sleep for centuries in order to refresh them.

Satan:
And, I concur with you.

Rabbi:
Do you sleep a lot?

Satan:
As much as you do.

Rabbi:

Is John in your hell?

Satan:

Not my place to tell you.

Rabbi:

Why not?

Satan:

Need to know, my friend. It's a need-to-know basis.

Rabbi:

I am onto something. Not sure how to get where I want, but I want clearer thinking and attainment of peaceful wisdom.

I want to overcome the astral plain. I want more understanding of death and what occurs on the other side of the veil of consciousness.

Satan:

You want the same thing God,
myself and all spiritual beings want.

Rabbi:

To me, that is amazing, that I am the same as God, s pirits and you.

Satan:

Why would that be a surprise to you?   Y ou see, none of us is perfect ...

Rabbi:

What about heaven and hell?
Do they exist on the other side of the veil?

Satan:

I guess, you have to die to find out.

Rabbi:

Thanks!!!! I am not going to push myself to find out.

Everything I put my hands onto, lately, deals with posterity leaving guides from ancient wisdoms.

I have the Emerald Tablets, the Gilgamesh Epic Tablets, Sumerian Enheduanna texts, the Egyptian Book Of The Dead, the Tibetan Book Of The Dead, then Homer, onward to the present day.

Fifteen billion years ago, my universe was formed - The Milky Way. That is:

1) our earth

2) our galaxy

3) our observable universe defined by the speed of light or sometimes referred to as the Hubble Volume or limits/edges of what we can see.

4) beyond the Hubble Volume is possibly stuff, energy, galaxies or a replication of our earth, galaxies, observable volumes.

5) beyond the Hubble Volume might be "Dark Flow" or massive structures or bizarre warps funneling gravitational forces from other universes.

6) beyond the Hubble Volume might be "Infinite Bubbles" with space expanding around the bubbles.

7) beyond the Hubble Volume might be "Black Hole Spawning" creating infinite new universes.

8) beyond the Hubble Volume might be "Many Parallel Universes" with our "String Theory" tying things together with dark matter and gravity.

Satan:
Beyond that, let's hope there is somebody who knows *something*. Lot of things God and I have never heard of or conceived.

Rabbi:
I do not know why I even talk to you, because you do not know shit-from-shinola, or your arse from a hole in the ground.

Satan:
Be careful! You seem to forget that I am as powerful as God.

Rabbi:
... and, apparently, as inept.

Rabbi Schlotz Talks With Satan: -Day 31

Rabbi:
Is the mind within the body or the body within the mind?

Satan:
You search in a state of confusion.

Rabbi:
I asked you a simple question: Are we a mind or body?

Satan:
Pinch yourself.

Rabbi:
In Tibet, certain adepts have influenced or left their teachings through other savants, such as W.Y. Evans-Wentz born 1878 died 1965.

He met with different people and tangentially aligned himself with Madam Helena Blavatsky's Theosophical Society, which is still in existence in California.

W. Y. Evans-Wentz disseminated Tibetan Buddhism through his translation of writings called: The Tibetan Book of the Dead with three other lesser translations called: Tibet's Great Yogi Milarepa, Tibetan Yoga Secret Doctrines, and fourthly: The Tibetan Book of the Great Liberation.

Satan:
I am faintly aware of these writings.

Rabbi:
Buddhism sees death as a form of cessation of consciousness in varying degrees of awareness.
Does consciousness move immediately to a new lifetime after death, or to some intervening period?

Satan:
The answer is dependent upon the level of awareness of the individual you are examining.

Rabbi:
So, all consciousness is individual?

Satan:
Of course.

Rabbi:
As an aside, the zillions of constellations and star groups within all of universes, leaves so much room for consciousness to choose from and inhabit or use?

Satan:
You answer your own question.

Rabbi:
How do you possibly keep track of all the souls in hell, with such a large area?

Satan:
That is not your concern. I don't have time to explain it to you.

Rabbi:

So, what are the possibilities of a soul after death or between bodies? Are we a body or a soul?

Satan:

Talking to you is like talking to a kindergarten student. Of course we are always a soul and sometimes a body.

Rabbi:

How, why, what, when and where?

Satan:

It, once more, depends upon the individual soul as to how these suppositions are answered.

For instance: You are in an intermediate space of a consciousness exploring the material world and conjecturing on the afterlife.

Rabbi:

I think I am pretty normal.

Satan:

Big deal! You are singularly insignificant. Your life and death are not a big thing to the history of time. You also are egotistically blind, and aware only slightly of the immensity of time. Third, you are just as normal as the next soul going in and out of time like traffic on a highway.

Rabbi:

I need to feel like I am making headway on increasing my spiritual awareness, because there is less to learn on the physical level.

Satan:

Keep on keeping on.

Rabbi Schlotz Talks With Satan: -Day 32

Rabbi:
(Interlude)

Church Lady

She's found at St Something
Backing up the priest of God
She has a fat husband, bling
He stopped giving her a nod

She's in the a room dark
Says she needs no light
Her eyes have a spark
As better heaven bright

Night she reads poems
To ease empty dreams
She lets fantasies roam
Through magic streams

When I look into her eyes
I project what she means
To my thought's desires
And my list of queens

I would never upset her
Nor play the rogue anon
From me there's no fear
She's safe, I'm no con

But who could refuse
This gentle lady true
Who takes away blues
Seals the deal for you

This world will but end
A sun will eat us up
Moon shadow bend
To blackness's cup

Flowers will all wilt
Green gardens go grey
Farmers will all quit
Plowing for their hay

Grocers' shelves empty
Potted plants dry dirt
But her love's aplenty
Worth more than a flirt

(End Of Interlude)

Rabbi Schlotz Talks With Satan: -Day 33

Satan:
You have a big thing on your mind. I will listen.

Rabbi:
My daughter, Susan:

I write to you with all the compressed love I have built up inside of me like an accordion that needs to be played if you would listen.

I cannot think of my past, before you were born, as anything but empty. I reached age twenty as a shell of a human being that needed a comet or rock from outer space to hit me on the head and drive me into a coma.

I was a bold ignorant child who saved himself from guns and danger in Detroit and in Vietnam, just for that night when they showed me you through the glass in Saint John's hospital with your fresh untouched bloom of a newborn baby. You, my daughter, who knew me thru the glass as sure as moths know the light they fly toward.

I looked at you and saw who you are now as an adult; that was an homage to me as your father, who cannot be swerved away from loving you as a core feeling deep as an ocean depth, as high as a distant star, as wide as an horizon in Alaska that has no sign of humanity stuck into pine trees and snow seemingly forever on each side of my eyes.

Can there ever be a time when I did not love you? Is the world too big to ever hold how I feel toward you? For years, I melted into rivulets from spring thaw. For years, I covered the forest with skunk cabbage and violets and trillium in green and purple shades.

Can there ever be anything as hard as the thin ironwood branches swinging in the breeze with their sturdy stubbornness? How can I touch you in your shell skin of bark, grown along an oak tree that never dies or gets old?

I miss you; as a swinging bush that a red wing black bird sat on and sang to heaven without even knowing what song it sang. But I sang adoration to you, my dearest daughter, of the infinite length and breadth of love.

I loved you; through your first marriage and kept the time sacred in my heart of every visit to you and your three children, as they grew up with my heart on how well you raised them. I loved you each time I attended their birthdays and celebrations of their growth.

I loved you when you divorced, and tried all I could to make sure the law was correctly put on your tax returns. I did my best. I never could have done anything better.

I loved you when you were leaving high school and we smoked marihuana on the roof of the house on the lake and fell asleep with blankets under the stars. How I felt about you being such perfection over all other children or all other mothers that I have ever known.

We changed. I remembered when my mother saw the look in my eye and yanked me out of the bath tub with her and locked the door, ending all the times we took baths together. She realized that I was suddenly a man and could no longer bathe with her. I cried and cried outside that door on the floor dripping wet, not understanding that my time had come to challenge the world, just as your time had come to challenge my love and put it into perspective.

There was nothing wrong with change between my mother and myself and between you and myself. These are growth things and are never meant to hurt each other.

I learned to make a life away from my mother and you have learned to make a life for yourself. We each grow a different branch on the tree of life and remain rooted to each other, as I still love my dead mother and still love my living daughter equally and with all the emotion that I can conjure up in love.

Susan, I adore you. I respect you. I am so proud of you beyond words. The last ten years, I decided that no matter what you thought or did, I would never ever change my living trust to give you, Scott, My sisters Anita and Grace equal shares of all my money and royalties from my books.

I idolize you more than my life, my books, my memories ...
I love you and always will, forever.

Yours for eternity.

Dad

Satan:

For once, I will be gracious. You have done well. I wish I could write like this.

Rabbi Schlotz Talks With Satan: -Day34

Rabbi:
Your place in history is tenuous, at best.
Devil worship or fear is rather new to the world.
For instance, exorcism was practiced centuries before
Christianity put your story on the wire. In fact, your story is one
of a God creating one man and one woman and their fall from
grace placing them upon an earth of pain and suffering.
Then, from this God's cadre, you challenge the God and are
thrown into a hell.

Satan:
So?

Rabbi:
How can one take you seriously?   You shout and throw fireballs
against the facts of history. What for?
Your Christian beginnings speak as if exorcism started with you,
but in ancient Mesopotamia, evil spirits entered a body and
were driven out by incantations and rituals of destroying a clay
or wax image of a demon.

Satan:
A wax image would not last too long in my home, ahah.

Rabbi:
Be serious.

Hindu religion has texts of Vedas of evil beings interfering with
the work of the Gods to harm the living.

In Persia, Zoroaster rituals used holy water to cast bad spirits out of a human body.

In the middle ages, demonology was considered a mental illness and barbaric treatments left much physical pain to patients.

Satan:

I will tell you this: people asked Rene Descartes: If you are a thing that thinks, then are you a dog or a horse as opposed to a human being? Descartes famous reply was: Why do I have to defend what I did **not** say I was? ... I am **The Devil** and that is all you need to know about me.

Rabbi Schlotz Talks With Satan: —Day 35

Rabbi:
I am tired of talking to you.

Satan:
Ditto. That goes double for me.

Rabbi:
You never give me opinions or advice. You are as closed mouth as a snake in the grass or a bat hanging upside down.

Satan:
Or a beetle bug? Why give advice to someone who knows everything?

Rabbi:
I am at a bit of a loss in reading so many things that seem to counter each other diametrically.

Satan:
Words lie.

Rabbi:
The emerald tablets speak of a soul who lived for 16,000 years. But, in thought, this soul decided after this length of time, to place himself under the rules of dying. Also, during this long life, he mostly slept.

Satan:
So?

Rabbi:
What nonsense. We all sleep to regenerate our strength. So do all souls on the other side of the veil. I suppose you sleep a lot?

Satan:
I am yawning, now.

Rabbi:
So, no matter what level of wisdom we reach, we always sleep. Hey! When we are born again, we are in a state of sleep until we reach some level of cognizance.

I read where there are "watcher" angels who protect our soul while we sleep? Is that true?

Satan:
Let's just say you wouldn't believe me if I told you. Why didn't you discuss that with God when you had the chance?

Rabbi:
Because you are more accessible; I can reach you when God is too busy.

Satan:
I should start charging you.

Rabbi:
What is your price?

Satan:
Just sign this contract.

Rabbi:
Go to hell. I am not selling my soul to you.

Satan:
Can't blame me for trying, though, it's not much of a soul ...

Rabbi:
Maybe if you wore a yarmulke and daven, like you were at the Wailing Wall in Jerusalem, I could take you more seriously.

Satan:
Isn't the character of someone enough? What has looks to do with anything? Besides, I have it on good authority that the Wailing Wall was not a remaining part of the temple of King David anyways.

Rabbi:
Yea? Well what was it? Something the Italian cement contractors built?

Satan:
Albanian cement contractors, if you must know.

Rabbi:
I want to ask you, is Pope Francis a fake?

Satan:
How do you mean? A prophet?

Rabbi:

It is purported that he is a Jesuit and that they have a plan for worldwide domination with the Pope ruling all the religions of the world as a savior, with dominion over alien intruders and all of humanity.

Satan:

Yea. So what? So many have tried to rule the world and look at what it got them. I oppose such an idea.

Rabbi:

In your case, attempted dominance got you put into hell.

Satan:

Leave me out of this discussion.

Rabbi Schlotz Talks With Satan: -Day 36

Rabbi:
Please look over these last three poems and give me your opinion.

Satan:
It might cost you.

Rabbi:
Please, or I will turn you over to Michael the archangel.

First poem:

tomorow has come

tomorrow has come
laid upon some
left over days

I recall her in her garden
as false ideas watered
and came alive for her
delusions. But she
does get credit
for trying to
outwit the
red wing
black bird
I filmed her forever in cameos
little scenes of severity

or admonishment
where all I could
get before she
passed in vain

Do not grieve but let the procession of flags pass
and say to whoever asks you:
How close where you to her? J
ust say: The second car.

Leave things as they are
because the sun lets in
all butterflies to eternity

Later a moon will remind us
that tomorrow will leave
and we will wake
remembering
we have left
our shoes
on the lawn
beneath a tree

Look for insects before
you slip them on to leave

Satan:
You do have a way with words.

Rabbi:
Second Poem:

porcelain eyes

porcelain eyes
porcelain moon
disturbed my heart
supple white smooth
porcelain streaked
my darkest eyes look into night

echoes of drums
faces of faded days
porcelain doll's glaze
heavy black confusion
puzzled cracks inside
where light left it's shadow
dim emptiness pulling me down
into footless paths of an indigo avenue

porcelain cries splinter silence
slivers of silver-glinted particles
she forms broken into loose sections
where memory is startled by shiny daggers

I slip between jagged branches
try to hide from piercing stabs

porcelain dangers strew themselves
upon winding lanes indistinct from sight

let hopeless pitch scenes dissapear
in a soul lost to grace

Michael Thomas 91

lost to love from
porcelain eyes

Satan:

I like how you use imagery, nicely done. I could do better. Will you listen to one of my poems? Roses are red, violets are ...

Rabbi:

It is not your turn yet.

Satan:

Pish!

Third Poem:

our lost prayers

our lost prayers
tell yourself it ain't over
time has not collapsed
into dark ages of light
where mysteries fall
tween cracks of believing

let yourself into closed doors
where familiar faces dissolve
and bones of ancient warriors
become smiling eyes of hope

tell me it is not done for good
we still have time for amending

all wasted mountains of dust
turned to pyrimads of stones

where pharoahs lay down their crooks and flails
take up beads of prayer for misunderstandings

we call out to valleys
we shout down rivers
let our voice envelope oceans
heard by sea creatures in their lairs
below blue waves undulating echoes

we all are pilgrims
forgetting our past
wishing some God
give missed answers
to all our lost prayers

Satan:
I have trouble with people who pray.

Rabbi:
It might do you some good. Try it.

Satan:
I prefer people who lose their temper and say: "Go to hell!"
Now, those are my kind of people.

Rabbi:

None of my family were put into a nut house.

My family was pretty well balanced.

If you put greed on one side and innocence on the other, my family was centered between the two.

It is not like they were very deep thinkers. But they were not insane. They were realists and very practical people.

My mother and father collected bread ties - a drawer full of these things that they may use one a year to keep the plastic tight. If I was to ask them what they were going to do with them, they would have no answer. But, after they died, it was me who emptied the drawer of them to put in the trash. I felt guilty for no reason whatsoever.

My parents paid all their bills and never borrowed money or owed a soul after they died.

An example of their shallow thinking, I once expounded on the theory of Einstein for about ten minutes. During a lull in my talking, my father looked at me and said: "Ain't that something." For all the intricacies of the theory of relativity, the most he could say was "Ain't that something."

He never read my first published work that I told him about and he said: "Well, you are on your way."

Satan:

Sounds like there were unresolved issues between you two?

Rabbi:
Less unresolved issues than great divisions in communication.

This must bore you, Mr Satan. But then, you have unresolved issues with your father, the God, whom you rejected.

Satan:
Leave that alone, please.

Rabbi:
If anyone in our family was crazy, it might be my aunt Mary. She was a childish person who stocked her cupboards with food that had developed mold.

My uncle Mike died in a gutter. He was alcoholic.

Satan:
I see … such hearty stock.

Rabbi Schlotz Talks With Satan: -Day 38

Rabbi:

Let's assume we can live forever. There are a whole slew of problems that erupt from that one premise.

First of all, no matter if we live for a short time or forever, we still have to come back because we are eternal, which has been proven over and over - ad nauseam.

So, if we have to come back in one-form-or-another, then all that matters is time and place between our departures and arrivals.

And, if time between can be measured, what difference does that measurement mean? It means nothing because the Buddha sat beneath a tree meditating till the tree ate him and he became part of the nutrients or soil for the roots of the tree.

Satan:

And a young disciple came, years later, to take a piss and the Buddha arose from the ground.

Rabbi:

You have heard the story?

Satan:

In one form or another. (*Snaps fingers*) Get on with your discussion or I will fall asleep listening to you.

Rabbi:

The most important element of living forever, or in various lifetimes, is that we have to sleep no matter what the situation is. You are **The Devil** and even you need to sleep as part of your nature. In fact, I have to pound my walking staff on the ground to wake you.

Satan:
That's more of a function of our conversations ... Gently, pound your walking staff. I am a tender soul.

Rabbi:
"Take us the foxes, the little foxes, which spoil the vines; for our vines have tender grapes."

Satan:
(Sarcastically) I am so glad you know scripture.

Rabbi:
The purpose of this discussion is that we sleep. We sleep no matter who, what, why, when or where. We sleep.

Satan:
You know, my erudite friend, sleep is a form of death.

Rabbi:
That is a whole other topic that we shall deal with eventually. Good night my friend.

Rabbi Schlotz Talks With Satan: -Day 39

Rabbi:
Death versus Sleep ... Do you want to start the discussion?

Satan:
You go right ahead ...

Rabbi:
To approach the subject we must start at the end or the "land of the dead"
Society or civilization begins with conjecturing on the end of life. All of humanity is obsessed by what happens when we die. Out of that question comes the land of the dead or the other side of the veil of life.
Is it a physical place?
Did Orpheus walk on a stable path, to bring his wife back from the dead?
I think we have a balanced belief that the "valley of death" can be a physical place or a spiritual place, but either way, souls in ether place must have stability. Souls can walk or float but need to be secure.

Satan:
You are starting very basic.

Rabbi:
Well, you are not giving me any clue. I have told you that I pound the ground with my walking stick to wake you up.

Satan:
Go on.

Rabbi:
In the land of the dead the occupants share each other's feelings about their existence, so it becomes a unifying place where souls complete themselves by comparing situations.

This valley of the dead is a stopping place for souls going either way: back to life or up to a new life.

Written on the stones of the Epic of Gilgamesh, the main character comes back from the dead to give his people salvation. In the Egyptian story of Toth, he lives for sixteen thousand years in the land of the dead and then accepts his own death to start a new life. His "Emerald Tablets of Toth" have survived for over 36,000 years. They speak of the land or place on the other side of life where souls can exist without bodily functions.

In the Odyssey, Odysseus passes through the land of the dead as part of his journey back to Penelope.

The land of the dead is described in both Gilgamesh and the Odyssey on the edge of the known world or beneath the world. Odysseus must have the help of Siduri to pass beneath Mt Mashu to reach the land of the dead.

Satan:
You know, I can read all this stuff myself.
Tell me something new.

Rabbi:
You are one of the most impatient people I have ever known.

Satan:
I am not just a person. I am a God and my time is valuable, you with your petty ego could never comprehend the value of eternity..

Rabbi:
You know that Odysseus spoke to his dead mother, Anticleia, who tells him how lonely she was waiting for him to return.
And, before he leaves, he speaks to Tiresias as well as one of his dead sailors. Odysseus is chided for not giving these dead souls a proper burial.
Also, Hercules had to fight his way retrieve the dog-of-hades as part of his twelve labors. While in hell, Theseus released him.
Aeneas entered hell to find the location of settling Rome by direction of his dead father Achises. Aeneas left and founded that place called Lavinium from which the people of Rome spring.
At some point in history, the land of the dead becomes hell. It becomes a haven for rest or a hellish punishment.
This is where you come in. Can souls leave your hell after some sort of redemption?

Satan:
I do not like to give forgiveness. That is my father's job. I get paid by the head count.
But, I will tell you the obvious: Whether the afterlife is a hell or a heaven, depends, mostly on the state of mind of the individual. Some find rest. Some find punishment. My fire can burn or put people to sleep.

Rabbi:
Is your rent remuneration based upon bodies or space?

Satan:
I do not like those damned squeamish residents bringing all their baggage *(mischievously)* I encourage only carry-on.

Rabbi:
Well now we live in huge cities and our grave yards are small places. In some countries where land is valuable, the dead are buried standing up to save space.
Older societies buried their dead, when they could afford it, with all their clothing, food and furniture that they would need on the other side.
Today, we throw pictures or memorabilia on top of the caskets or inside of them before the dirt covers them up.

Satan: *(shrugs shoulders disinterestedly.)*

Rabbi Schlotz Talks With Satan: -Day 40

Rabbi:
I have a silly poem. Sorry for waking you.

rambling

when they opened me up
this is what they found
my internal organs
were tightly bound

my ears could not listen
membranes unglisten
stubbornness of tissue
scapulos deep fisures

they tied a sales tag
to the zip up bag
so that inventories
stayed below forties

my heart opened up
blood dried in a cup
liver unremarkable
measured with skill

I have to tell you this
you would not want to kiss
my lips sewn so shut
they stitched up my gut

I was not taxidermied
nor wired in a hurry
I was not even buried
toasted crematoried

I could never return
no longer did I learn
I was brain dead
silenced instead

so take time my friend
eternity has no end
you can't smell asters
out of urns of plasters

horses keep on running
expressways humming
night 's empty streets
where ghosts all meet

door to heaven is open
basements down to hell
so keep praying hoping
that God will be your pal

no one leaves earth alive
you work eight to five
save coins in a cup
sleep just interrupts

voices you remembered
Maggie died in December
drank beer ate hamburger
till her eyes became blurred

my dad died coughing
with nurses all laughing
my mother smoked relaxing
till cancer took her gasping

my brother lost his appetite
his colon wound too tight
for food to be passing
his digestion never lasting

all my aunts and uncles
were laid to-rest in bundles
my ancestors cemeteries
are all distant memories

I never needed therapy
I've always been happy
I talk to hide my fear
my mind will stay clear

my ex-wives say I'm crazy
my future is not so hazy
I work hard save my money
to me life is just funny

I eat and sleep with ease
do just what i please
my doctor hears my rant
my teeth are all implants

I clean my own floors
wipe stains off doors
dust around corners
avoid all mourners

I am really not a poet
my writing is trickery
I would trade stale donuts
for words that are slippery

do not take what I say
read the bible your way
Egyptian book of the dead
will just screw up your head

you do not need to be reborn
there is no heaven or hell
the Buddha is just snoring
till he hears the temple bell

Confucius spread his religion
saying obey your government
love your neighbor is confusing
sleep till you learn what it meant

this is all I have to offer
from wisdom I abstain
my cloak and dagger
hide me from sun or rain

Satan: *(Yawns through half closed eyes and falls asleep again)*

Rabbi Schlotz Talks With Satan: -Day 41

Rabbi:
Trying something different: This is my Requiem.

Requiem by Rabbi Schlotz

In beginning silver smooth tenderness encompassed all aspects of earth and its starry place in universality.

There were delicacies in all deliberations that were impervious to decay. Every tidbit of panorama lay enfolded within its primordial skin.

Fingers touched protuberances of stalactites and stalagmites. Eyes could be seen within the shimmer of walled horizons drawn down flat to a round shadowed star-sky full of boundless mysteries.

Any requiem must have its beginning in an imperishable life. We cannot mourn what never existed. We can only feel detachment from differentiation. If you are, then you cannot be. If banquets lay before us then starvation hovers.

The tinge of ink spreads throughout liquid of loveliness. One bad apple spoils the whole bunch. I sit beneath the pear tree. Bugs, flies, ants, worms crawl inside and out of the burnished fruit and my heart feels gladness for such special disgusting disintegration.
I feel the diminishing pale pulp of life reducing itself to death.

This reality - this universe abounds with such magnitudes of horror and equal beauty. Side-by-side examples of both keep in-tuned hearts hovering between serenity and insanity.

If you examine examples, think about the creep who meets you at his door for the first time and wants immediately to steal from you with his furnace eyes. Even from a short distance, one can smell his sulfur breath and feel darkness stretched around him like barnacles attached to his sunken soul.

He says his name is Ed and asks if I have a coffee table for him. I tell him that I do not. I inform him that I bought two lawn chairs for him and the other people in his building. He does not say thanks. He only asks if he can take the lawn chairs into his apartment to use. I am amazed and tell him, no! They are for the porch and for everyone. He says. It is too cold to sit outside. I tell him that spring is coming and winter will soon be gone. It does not register with him and he returns to asking me for a coffee table as he points to the empty spot in his living room.

All I can think about is getting away from this rat-of-a-man. He is some kind of bug-under-a-rock that I wish I never turned over.

Satan: *(Feigns snoring)*

But, this is a requiem for this demented soul as he lives in a building with Mary who is so precious and kind. Mary who offers you casseroles and says thanks for the gifts I have given her.
This is a requiem for life in its complexities. Life is in the balance. And, when the forces of nature eat away at the fringes

of time, these comparisons will wash away forever to leave a vacancy within space that mourns both evil and goodness.

I cannot dream life to be any better than sorrow. I am sure that if there was a Jesus hanging on a cross as a sacrifice to sin. It is my bet that he was the saddest angel ever. He probably looked through the pain of humanity and saw despair. People do not change. Souls do not become good overnight. Jesus could be told the words that Bob Dylan wrote in a song called "The Man In The Long Black Coat" which were "People don't live or die. People just float."

No one can say it any better for this requiem. People just float. This is a dirge for people floating. This is my requiem. And, I stand at the greying monument of a sandstone chipped angel with broken wings and wasted eyes. I hear deep in the center of this statute, a cry for life in the balance.

A side story about nothing:

From Teresa:

You once asked what I see in you -

you are a delightful gentleman, in an era I thought chivalry would never return, who occasionally exhibits a rough edge and is willing to laugh at himself, available to help others instantly and also encourages others, is grateful, generous, creative, talented, very knowledgeable, insightful, witty, resourceful, passionate especially re: values, truth, honesty & for those unable to speak for themselves in society, an uplifting optimist, a loyal friend/supervisor, a cat lover, has the courage to speak what's on his mind - boldly if needed - is fiercely independent, appreciates classical music, shares willingly to his last cent if circumstances require, contributes to making this world better through his actions and thoughtful writings as a published author and a joy to be in his presence

are some of the traits I appreciate and love in you, Michael.

Back To: Teresa:

I am falling into the well of your love
Rope will no longer help me out
I hear and read all the things you say
I stand back and say maybe, but it scares me
I try so hard to keep learning
And I know that self-adulation is a detriment
So, please excuse me for saying this:

I am a fool with a coconut brain
I have no idea how God endures me
I am a resurrected Lazarus of Bethany
Who tells Jesus, now I have to die all over
Lazarus's sisters made him do the dishes and clean house
He told them that he was reborn and needed a rest

A crabby old man lived in a cave writing:
"If you have two shirts in the closet, one belongs to you and the other to the man who has no shirt"

I say: "If you have two shirts in the closet they both belong to men who have no shirts, because God will keep me clothed with leafs and ferns"

St Jerome wrote the Vulgate
Church ladies brought bread and wine to his cave
And church ladies brought him scrolls from the library and they took back scrolls that he was done reading
There was one church lady that he fell in love with and he built a monastery for himself and added a wing for her to live so she was there at night when he got horny

Satan: *(Hand gestures a gun in his mouth firing)*

Because the people of the town begin to criticize him, he built another monastery nearby and started a nunnery convent for only woman
He gave his church lady an appointment as the abbesses in charge and rode a donkey to her monastery each night to sleep with her

People in the town said: "We are not sure if St Jerome is the donkey or the donkey is St Jerome
It is time-within-time spreads itself over eternity.

Say the word: "ZIN-URU" and repeat it to release the power in sound.
I hear the mystery inside of the word and I begin to live the word with its vibrations of sound that bathe me in wisdom and lead me deeper into the light of the star spaces.

Pray to our brothers seven who protect us from the darkness of night: UNTANAS / QUERTAS / CHIETAL / GOYANA / HUERTAL / SEMVETA / ARDAL.

3=Untanas = dark power, key of all magic, underworld.

4=Quertas loosens power, frees souls

5=Chietal master of all

6=Goyana lord of light, hidden path

7=BHuertal lord of space and time

8=Semveta progress, judges

9=Ardal Father

Horlet is master of Unal

By their names I implore thee, free me from darkness and fill me with LIGHT.

Rabbi Schlotz Talks With Satan: -Day 42

Rabbi:
I have devoted this sixteenth book to discussion with you. Much of the time I get very little response from you. I have come to the definite conclusion that you exist as some lower form of the dark light and you do not like the role you play.

Satan:
You are one of the most astute souls I have ever encountered. I am sure I would love to have you in hell permanently just for the conversation.

Rabbi:
I wish I could enjoin you, but I have greater things to think out. If you stay with me for the balance of this book, try to release your imagination and work with me.

Satan:
Okay

Rabbi:
I am torn between being a human being and striving to overcome human things like hunger, sex, depression, elation or death. The wealth of information I have at my disposal lends itself to spiritualism and that encompasses loving my neighbor and loving some invisible God.

Satan:
My father God? He's not exactly invisible; you can only see him from certain perspectives.

Rabbi:
I do not believe he or she is just your father. I think you just made up the break with your higher forces so that you can have individuality as a force of evil.

I do not think you are that evil. Proof of that is you do not even want to talk to other souls in hell. You find them boring.

Satan:
True.

Rabbi:
You are not helping me with growing spiritually. You say you have some familiarity with the "The Emerald Tablets of Thoth"

Satan:
Yes:

Rabbi:
Let me tell you this: Spirituality has an agenda. There are first the general rules of some superior being and secondly there are the various paths a person can take in real life to achieve some of the goals. Now, those paths are not laid out or proscribed in detail because they depend upon the attitude or mind of the aspirant.,

Satan:
That makes sense.

Rabbi:

Yet, the paths a person takes are detailed in that they contain a main theme of overcoming the body and rising to higher levels of consciousness.

In my first attempts to achieve greater spirituality, I worked with people who proscribed meditating and praying through the colors of the rainbow.

There were other prayers less central to the rainbow:

> Oh ruby red color of life
> flowing richly through me
> energize me revitalize me
> recharge my will and stamina

> warming orange float in me
> restore my will my conscious energy
> lifting orange transmuting rays
> awake my budding powers
> bring wisdom to my hours

> flowing saffron beams of gold
> bring forth in me pure joy
> golden atoms digest all wisdom
> all fear in me destroy

> oh ray of emerald symphony
> sustain up build my wayward heart
> its strings attune in symphony
> teach me to do my part

oh chlorophyll builder true
heart force in fields and man renew
from thee the temple true is bidden

oh tranquil ray of sapphire blue
calm thou my mind in solace new
quench thou all fevers in cool refreshing dew
tone thou my speech and make it true
help me to learn to rest in you
help me to learn to speak anew
help me to learn to sing in you

oh zenith ray of violet power
cleanse my blood with purple shower
soothe thou my nerves with passions lower
bring forth true inspirations flower
oh amethyst ray of spirits radiance
bring forth the poetry, music, fragrance

Satan:
Nice prayer. But, as I've said, I like people who do not pray but
say: "Go to hell".   Those are my favorite people.

Rabbi:
The emerald tablets were written 16,000 years ago by a soul
called Thoth or "Thrice-greatest Hermes" who lived for 36,000
years and then willed himself to die to go to another level of
spiritualism. Thoth or Hermes states emphatically that he will
return to judge his adherents who may have disobeyed his
strictures. Before he died he says he built the great pyramid of
Cheops and installed room after room leading up to the pinnacle

where he had kept in safety, the sayings of his teachings. In time those sayings were inscribed on the emerald tablets which have a substance unknown to science even today.

The tablets were moved to the pyramid in Mexico for safety and then left forgotten after the Spanish invaders conquered the natives.

 In reading those tablets an important fact emerges: That Hermes and all the souls in the afterlife all sleep.

Satan:
We all sleep. Even the God sleeps.

Rabbi:
Sleep has layers of protection to keep the soul safe from dark forces.

The second thing from the Tablets is some form of guardians called the seven lords of amenti.

Amenti is the home of all souls who exist in the white light.

The seven lords are numbered (I do not know why they start with three)

3: Untanas or the lord of the underwoeld and magic
4: Quertas or the lord of power
5: Chietal or lord master of all
6: Goyana or lord of light
7: Huertal or lord of space and time
8) Semvata or lord of progress. Judge
9) Ardal or father
Horlet is master of Unal

Satan:
You know, my friend, all we do is talk about your futile search for spirituality. Now, it is my turn to talk about eternal rewards.
I can offer you so many things that you never have considered.
I am as powerful as God and a hell-of-lot nicer.
I can offer you eternity that you fight so hard to obtain.
You can live forever in my home.
As soon as you get settled in your home, I will show you the remote control by which you can open the garage door, close the patio door, set the toaster or oven, and best of all: control the temperature in your palatial house in hell.

Rabbi:
You are kidding?

Satan:
Not one bit. Plus you will have a chauffeur and Rolls Royce waiting in your garage all hours of the night and day. And, you can take the Pacific Coast Highway or the Ice fields Parkway in Canada and forever drive with a bottle of wine and potato chips. Not only that, but you will have any women or number of woman to pull over on the side of the road and get-it-on, with. No strings.
And, there is more.

Rabbi:
I am listening.

Satan:

The potato chips have cheese!

I have roadside restaurants and motels that all are free without you even having to register with invasive desk clerks asking you questions.

Rabbi:

I suppose you have ice machines at the end of the hallway?

Satan:

You bet.

Rabbi:

I do not think I am interested because I know you will knock on the door and hand me a contract to sign selling my soul to you.

Satan:

I promise to leave you alone for as long as you want. Forever is a long time to get drunk and have a different lady each night.

Rabbi:

You seem to forget that I have a wife: Mrs Rabbi.

Satan:

I promise to console her.

Hey! I will throw in an insurance policy that will make her rich, after you are declared dead by the courts.

Rabbi:

And my children?

Satan:

No problem. You have two, and I will be sure they are rich too.

Rabbi:

I am still not interested.

Satan:

Wait. If you act now, I will add a double gift of ownership in the largest diamond mine in Africa and I will increase the stones that your workers will chip out of the rock.

Rabbi:

You are funny.

Satan:

Not funny but real. Tell me what you want.
I think I know what you want.
You want access to the Library in Alexandria before it was destroyed. I will give you the ability to go to any library in the world at any time in history.   That includes the New York Public Library, The George Peabody Library in Baltimore, The Bodleian Library in Oxford. All of them any time you want. I will include a hot plate and hundreds of cases of Campbell soup.

Rabbi:

Cream of mushroom?

Satan:

Certainly! Any variety.

Rabbi Schlotz Talks With Satan: -Day 44

Rabbi:
Conquer by silence the bondage of words
Let thy mouth speak into the ether
Give thy thoughts freedom of air
In full your words speak emptiness
Little beams of sparks come forth
Out of tongues of fire
First steps began an everlasting journey
Time turns into itself in metamorphoses
Balloons of escapism burst into nights calm
Let darkness pass into songs of shadows
A psalm of sorrow unfolds into joy
Let shadows merge with sleeping light
We are messengers of stillness
Look upon our eyes fixed with love
There you will find all answers
Treasure goodness only for itself
Rewards of wisdom make the wise man
    a magnet for all light and joy

Research: *(This is only research for my next story or poem. This is the voice of Thoth of the emerald tablets.)*

"I began preaching to people the beauty of religion and knowledge. "O people, men born on the Earth, who indulge in drunkenness, sleep, and the ignorance of God! Sober up, cease your surfeit, awake from your dullness!
"Why do you give up yourselves to death while you have power to partake of immortality?

"Depart from the dark path, be partakers of immortality, abandon forever your vices!

"Nowhere but in God can you find good!"

(From **Hermes**' address to the Egyptians)

"Atlantis was an archipelago consisting of two large islands situated in the Atlantic Ocean near the Mediterranean Sea. There existed a highly developed civilization of the Atlanteans. The most important point about this civilization is that it possessed the true religious-philosophical knowledge, which allowed many people to advance quickly in their development — up to the Divine level — and accomplish thus their personal human evolution.

However, with time Atlantis' spiritual culture degraded, and as a result the power in the country was taken over by aggressive people, who preferred black magic and domination over others rather than the principle of the true spiritual development. Then God made the islands of Atlantis sink into the ocean.

But the higher spiritual knowledge was preserved by some Atlanteans, Who achieved Divinity. They brought it into Egypt and other countries, where this knowledge existed for some time providing a basis for the local spiritual culture.

About the Emerald Tablets*

In the Emerald Tablets, Thoth-the-Atlantean explains the reason for the destruction of Atlantis: confidential knowledge was imparted to unworthy people and the latter began using it for evil purposes. They also adopted bloody sacrifices — and this resulted in numerous incarnations of hellish beings among people.

When the destruction of Atlantis happened (two islands submerged into the ocean one after another according to the Divine Will), Thoth-the-Atlantean moved to Egypt (Khem) with a group of other Divine Atlanteans.

The Primordial* advised Thoth thus: "Go forth as a Teacher of men! Go forth preserving the records (with Teachings) until in time the Light grows among men!

"Light* shall You be all through the ages, hidden yet found by enlightened men. For working on all the Earth, give We You power, free You to give it to others or take it away."

And then Thoth worked as a Representative of the Primordial.

... Thoth relates that He went the entire Path to Mergence with the Primordial. He writes that anyone can traverse this Path. The Path necessarily contains obstacles, which create difficulties for travelers: these difficulties prevent weak, ethically unworthy, or intellectually immature people from going further. "Go! But do not take with you the unwise, insincere, weak!" says Thoth.

Thoth gives basic recommendations for initial harmonization of the chakra system. For fulfilling just these recommendations He promises health and longevity.*

On the higher stages of meditative practices (i.e. on the stage of Buddhi Yoga), one has to dive with the consciousness into the

Depths of the multidimensional space and cognize there "star worlds" and the Light of the Great Fire on the Path to the Abode of the Primordial*. There are also other spatial dimensions, which are "vacant to all seeming, yet hidden within them are the keys..."*

Thoth also explains one of the higher meditations — the Temple and its particular variation — the Pyramid.

About the history of His own spiritual ascent, Thoth says the following:

"Once in a time long forgotten, I, Thoth, opened the doorway, penetrated into other spaces and learned of the secrets concealed.

"Often did I journey down the dark pathway unto the space where the Light ever glows.

"Long then dwelt I in the Temple of the Primordial until at last I was One with the Light."

Later Thoth embodied Himself again in Egypt and was Hermes Trismegistus (Thrice-born)*.

Thoth gives the following directions to spiritual seekers:

Preserve and keep the command of the Primordial One:
Look in your life for disorder and get rid of it! Balance and order your life!

Quell all the chaos of emotions and you shall have harmony in life.

Conquer by silence the bondage of words.

Keep ever your eyes on the Light!

Surely when you deserve it, you shall be one with your Master! And surely then you shall be one with the All*!

Know My commandments! Keep them and fulfill them, and I will be with you, helping and guiding you into the Light!

Out of the darkness shall you raise upward, one with the Light!

Man has to strive to become the "Divine Sun".

Follow this Path and you shall be One with the All!

Light comes only to those who strive. Hard is the Pathway that leads to the Wisdom; hard is the Pathway that leads to the Light. Many stones shall you find in your pathway, many mountains shall you climb towards the Light.

Man, know that always beside you walk the Messengers of Light. Open to all is Their Pathway, to all who are ready to walk into the Light!

Suns are They, Messengers of Light to shine among men. Like man are They, and yet are unlike.

Know that many dark shadows shall fall on your light* striving to quench with the shadows of darkness the light of the soul that strives to be free. Many the pitfalls that lie on this Way, seek ever to gain Greater Wisdom! Cognize — you shall know the Light!

Light is eternal and darkness is fleeting. Seek ever, O man, for the Light! Know ever that as Light fills your being, darkness for you shall soon disappear!

Open the soul to the Messengers of Light! Let Them enter and fill you with Light!

Keep ever your face to this Goal!

... Open the soul, O man, to the cosmos and let it "flow" through you as one with the soul!*

Man's evolution consists in the process of changing to forms that are not of this world. Grows he in time to the formless — to live on a higher plane. Know that you must become formless before you can be one with the Light.

Listen, O man, to My voice, telling of pathways to Light, showing the way of attainment: how you shall become one with the Light:

Search first the mysteries of the Earth's Heart! Seek the Flame* of the Living Earth! Bathe in the glare of this Flame!

Know, O man, you are complex, a being of matter and of Fire. Let your Flame* shine out brightly! Be you only the Flame!

Seek ever more Wisdom! Find it in the Heart of the Flame! Know that only by your striving can Light pour into you!

Only the one, who of Light has the fullest, can hope to pass by the guards of the Way, who prevent unworthy people from entering it.

You shall cognize yourself as Light and make yourself ready to pass on the Way.

Wisdom is hidden in darkness. When shining with Soul-Flame, find you the Wisdom, then shall you be born again as Light, and then shall you become the "Divine Sun".*

Grow into One with the Light! Be a channel of Divine Principles to the world of men!

Seek, O man, to find the great Pathway that leads to eternal Life — through the image of the "Divine Sun"!

… Know, O man, you are only a soul! The body is nothing! The soul is everything! Let not your body be a fetter!

Cast off the darkness and travel in Light! Learn to cast off your body, O man, and be free from it!* Become the true Light and unite then with the Great Light!*

Know that throughout space the eternal and infinite Consciousness exists. Though from superficial knowledge It is hidden, yet still forever exists.

The key to these Higher worlds is within you; it can be found only within.*

Open the gateway within you, and surely you, too, shall live the true life!

... Man, you think that you live... but know that your former life can bring you only to death. For as long as you are bound to your body, no true life exists for you! Only the soul which is free from the material world has life which is a really true life! All else is only a bondage, a fetter from which to be free!

Think not that man is born for the earthly! Though born on the Earth, man is a light-like spirit! Yet, without true knowledge, man can never become free!

... Darkness surrounds the souls seeking to be born in Light. Darkness fetters souls... Only the one who is seeking may ever hope for Freedom!

Let you be the "Divine Sun" of the Great Light! Fulfill this and you shall be free!

The Great Light that fills all the cosmos is willing to help you, O man! Make you of your body a torch of Light that shall shine among men!

... Hear and understand: the Flame is the source of all things; all things are its manifestation!

Seek to be One with the "Divine Sun"!

Hold your thought on uniting the Light with your human body.

Light is the Source of all the life; for without the Great Light nothing can ever exist!

Know, Light is the basis of all formed matter.

Know, O man, that all space is filled by worlds within worlds.

Deep beneath the image of the Pyramid lies My secret. Seek and find it in the Pyramid I built.

Follow this key I left for you. Seek and the doorway to the true Life shall be yours! Seek in My Pyramid deep beneath it, and in the Wall.*

Know that it is in the Pyramid I built that you shall find the secret way into the true Life.

... Seek and find there That Which I have hidden! There shall you find the "underground entrance" to the secrets hidden before you were men.
Know We that of all, nothing else matters except the growth of the soul. Know We the flesh is fleeting. The things men count great are nothing to Us. The things We expect from you are not of your bodies but are only the perfected state of the souls.

When you can learn that nothing but progress of the soul can count in the end, then truly you are free from all bondage, free to work in accordance with your predestination!

Know, O man, you are to aim at Perfection, for only thus can you attain to the Goal!

Know that the future is never in fixation but follows man's free will! Man can only "read the future" through the causes that bring the effects in destinies.

Know that your body when in perfect balance may never be touched by the finger of death! Aye, even "accidents" may only approach when you abandon your predestination! When you are in harmony with your predestination, you shall live on in time and not taste of death.

... Know you not that in the Earth's Heart is the source of harmony of all things that exist and have been on its face? By the soul you are connected with the Earth's Heart, and by your flesh — with the matter of Earth.

When you have learned to maintain harmony in yourself, then shall you draw from the harmony of the Earth's Heart. Exist then shall you while Earth is existing, changing in form, only when Earth, too, shall change: tasting not of death, but one with this planet, living in your body till all pass away.

... Three are the qualities of God in His Light-Home*: Infinite Power, Infinite Wisdom, Infinite Love.

Three are the powers given to spiritual Masters: to transmute evil, to assist good, to use discernment*.

Three are the things They manifest: Power, Wisdom, and Love.

Three are the Manifestations of Spirit creating all things: Divine Love possessing the perfect knowledge, Divine Wisdom knowing all possible means of helping living beings in their development, Divine Power which is possessed by the Primordial Consciousness Whose essence is Divine Love and Wisdom.

Darkness and Light are both of one nature, different only in seeming, for each arose from one Source. Darkness is chaos. Light is Divine Harmony. Darkness transmuted is Light.

This, My children, is your purpose in being: transmutation of darkness into Light!

Rabbi Schlotz Talks With Satan: -Day 45

Satan:

What's on your mind?   Why did you wake me?

Rabbi:

I woke you because you are lazy. You sleep too damn much.

Satan:

You are a megalomaniac. I do not pass judgment upon you while you sleep, and I am a God.

Rabbi:

It is a fact that you are so guilt free that you can sleep at the drop of an anvil.

Satan:

Or the drop of a feather.

Rabbi:

We live our lives of mundane activities. We waste away with pain and hidden sorrows and pass from the earth leaving very little remembrance of us.
We, in the majority, try to be kind to all we come into contact with. We try to be generous, never hanging onto material things.
We try so hard to retain only the spiritual things like appreciation for nature and all of God's gifts.

Satan:
I have promised you so much more than what God gives you.

Rabbi:
With strings.

Satan:
God has strings. You have to obey or you get damned to hell.

Rabbi:
Well, at least you have a purpose, when you wake up.

Satan:
If you have nothing more to say, I am going back to bed.

Rabbi:
Why are we beset with such alternating urges?   Be spiritual yet youth and sex and drugs urge us equally.
We touch a dollar and we feel greed for more.
We give and wait for something to be given to us.
I do not want to do evil things, but you really make it easy for us to steal and degrade our behavior.
It seems that the evil path is easier than the path of goodness.

Satan:
Thank you. I do a pretty good job at it.

Rabbi:
Master deceiver.

Satan:

You know, it is not my place to tell you this, but I will step out of my role for telling you that it takes as much energy to do good as it does to do evil. It only requires more wisdom.

Rabbi:

That is amazing. Why would one chose to do evil, then?

Satan:

I do not want you to repeat what I just said, but I pray for all the souls in heaven to do evil.

Rabbi:

You pray?

Satan:

Damn right. How in the hell do you think I get things done? I pray for all the lovely bad and evil things that people can do.

Rabbi:

Prayer infers a point of holiness.

Satan:

Not by my measurement. What do you think all the souls in hell do? They pray. Besides, I almost never have to worry. Souls come into my hell by the dozens and thousands. My waiting room is always busy.

Rabbi:

Those people pray out of regret.

Satan:

So what? They pray to me to let them go.

Rabbi:

You know, mister, the souls in hell all have the inner power to release themselves.

Satan:

Yea! But they haven't reached a level of wisdom to realize it.

Rabbi:

Amazing! It seems so easy.

Satan:

Not really. You cannot expect every person that checks out in the supermarket stores to all have wisdom. Just look at some of the crap that stupid people buy.
And, just look at where that crap finds its way into the weekly garbage pickup.
I, frankly, love those ignorant people, because I see them as viable prospects to get them in hell when they die.

Rabbi:

Do any of the people in hell work their way out of hell on their own?

Satan:

I get tired of you asking such dumb questions. There are converted damn souls who leave hell, but I have nothing to do with their change of minds. They sneak bibles into hell and read with flashlights under their blankets. They think I do not see them. I leave them alone because there are too few for me to bother with. Now, you! I am willing to bet that your inflated ego. Your misconception that you are elevated, kind or holy, might just be your downfall.

Remember the very first sentence of the Iliad by Homer. He says he is going to tell us how the pride of Achilles brings about his death. Oh! You know time is "thin" and I am still in negotiations with God over Achilles.

Rabbi:

I am not going to brag, but I know I am a good person.

Satan:

You would not believe the millions upon millions of clueless souls who have said that before you. It's just the attitude I love.

Rabbi Schlotz Talks With Satan: -Day 46

Rabbi:
A love interlude

If I fail to love you
In error by oversight
Miss calling you oceans
Flowers lilting loveliness

Overlook my blinking
Blind colors of your light
Where rainbows spill
Down rain swept tears

Do not fret if absentmindedly
My knees forget to genuflect
My hands do not fold in prayer
Trumpets call your passing carriage

I am sure I was inattentive
For magic of sleight hand
Moves too slow for your eyes
Rumors fade to blind hearts

Give me second chance
Ancient flutes enchant
Valley church vespers
Invite tolling shadows
My tender heart open
For what blessed grace

Wraps my sorrows
Prayers take me up

You in your goodness
Can only be called
Across night shade
Into morning glade

Where I wait
Harps, stones
Wake me to
Your kiss

Rabbi Schlotz Talks With Satan: -Day 47

Rabbi:

I will make you a deal. You sign an agreement with me to pledge your soul only to salvation and I will work with you to get you out of hell and back into the graces of God.

Satan:

(Mockingly Excited) Ohhh, a deal! I am listening.

Rabbi:

There are two layers to existence.

One, you get reborn over and over till you reach some layer of spiritualism or understanding and you are finished with the reincarnation cycle.

Two, you learn to overcome death and exist without the body in a state of spiritualism or understanding and become a teacher or adept.

Satan:

OK. Where's the deal?

Rabbi:

With your help, we both will reach levels that will allow us to preach and convert all the souls in hell to a more balanced existence. We are very lucky to have our parish set in place without having to start from scratch and be able to begin our heaven quicker.

God will let us alone, because he will be happy that the forces of evil will slowly be changed to forces of good.

Satan:

You make things sound so easy.

Rabbi:

If something is complicated then it is not worth its weight in gold.

You know, it is time for you to make a change. The old idea of a hell raising devil using his wiles to entrap souls into damnation - that concept is just outdated.

You, as **The Devil**, are like the Jews who still are waiting for the messiah. What fools the Jews are. They embody the wasted principle that: "It is better to wait than to admit that he has arrived."

You see: The Jews are lazy. For them to admit that Jesus was the messiah, they would have to give up all the posturing of being the chosen people.

What bunk. God did not choose them. They were so delirious walking around in the desert heat as lost tribes. The Jewish bakers had to work all night making bread and spreading it around the ground at night. When morning came, the half-crazed people ate the bread and proclaimed that God sent them manna from heaven. Meanwhile, the big fat bakers tried to get some sleep for the next evenings work making more bread.

You, Satan, are like the Jews. Your time has come to divest yourself of the image of evil. From the minute you wake up till you go back to sleep, you are running around hell scaring the shit out of souls who are screaming for water. You would do much better selling those people bottled water and set up recycle bins for them to put the empty plastic bottles.

I think the problem you have is you do not know how to accept love. You can only accept fear. It takes a brave soul to know how to receive love. In order for you to learn acceptance, you would have to learn to give love back - quid-pro-quo.

Satan:
You really think you know everything.

Rabbi:
I think that you are lazy. You take the easy way out by pretending to be evil incarnate.   The harder path would be to kneel to God and use your powers for good.
 Your time has come to introduce yourself as the "New and improved" Satan. You need to love. You need to face the world as God's greatest angel of love. If you want to be the top banana, you got to start from the bottom of the pack. If you want to rise to the surface, you need to stir the pot.

Satan:
You think **I** have problems? *(Laughs maniacally)*

Rabbi Schlotz Talks With Satan: -Day 48

Rabbi:
A letter *to her:*

I am entertaining thoughts of avoiding you for some future time/months, again.
I do this to most all of the relationships I have ever had.
It is something in me that keeps me satisfyingly independent.
I am well aware of the fact that you stricture me to never go away again.
I play a balancing act within me. An analysis of you:

1) I fell in love with you the moment I met you and you promised to pray for me.

2) I recognized you as a person of consistency, a soul of higher spirituality than others

3) I evaluated you as an obtainable person - one that I would learn from and one that I could manipulate without oppressing.

4) An important feature of your character is that you are a person who serves others.

5) You are estimable. You are the only person in the whole world who has pinpointed me successfully and epitomized my nature. In one paragraph you sized me up in writing and I was taken aback by your astute observations.
6) What do I get out of my relationship with you?

7) You are like a high school mentality of innocence and would conduct yourself or be happy with an abstemious relationship like tea-and-crumpets or Alice in Wonderland impervious distancing.

8) I, on the other hand, am a hot blooded, tear away the facade and touch the secret juices of a woman between her breasts and between her divided legs of pleasure. I am a pirate of pleasure. I am a cannibal. The pure animal Caliban, that Shakespeare describes in the Tempest play, the wild man who is untamed and takes what he wants without censor.

Be sure to understand that my distinctions are fraught with error or conciseness, both at once.

In my whole life there was only one other person that I met who was better than me, like you are. That person was above me spiritually and I realized her nature long after I went about my life meeting inadequate people. She was too good, as you are, for my state of being. I briefly touched with her and never established any kind of juncture with her. But, I do harbor regret that I could never have come up to her standards, just as I feel about you. You are greater than me in so many ways.

I go on-and-on, like a man who is out of control. But, you are married with children and have a place in life that is established and secure. You, my dear, would have too much to lose by having an excursion with my dissembling balance. I would be **The Devil** to you saintliness. It does not matter what your evaluation of yourself is, because you have an unjustifiable negative opinion of yourself that does not match the real you that I see.

I am pretty terrible with this in-depth writing and I do not have the right to be this frank with you. My epistle violates the boundary of courtesy and for that I apologize.

As a writer, I have maintained such standards that sometimes are impossible to keep.

My first wife was so far below me that I almost cannot believe how base I was to marry her since she never came close to understanding me or herself. She remains that way to this day.

My second wife turned out to be a taker. You, by the way, are a giver.

My relationship with Patricia for thirty five years was one where I superficially established her as a pseudo wife, though we never shared sex or title since she had a husband and she also was a taker, but I allowed her to take. My reasons for her being part of my life was for me to give her all the money and attention that I did out of love for her without needing her to give back to me. I used her as the recipient of my unconditional ability to love.

When God took her away from me, I "re-centered" myself ideologically, continuing to be the self-styled solitary amoeba, one celled structure, which I always am.

So, what do I get from you?

The main reason I continue with you is that you are superior to me. But, it is tenuous and I am not sure how long it will last.

I do love you. I do not know how I would act around you in an extended way. I am totally sure I could make it work, but I would have to become better than I am. I would have to make the lie-of-me, the truth-of-me.

I project that my feelings of reductive semblances will win over, eventually.

I just never can be the right gas to power your motor.

Satan:
You are so invasive with you reductive reasoning. Why on Earth would you have such faith in your judgments, knowing their track record?

Rabbi Schlotz Talks With Satan: -Day 49

Rabbi:

Discourse of discontent

Mercy be kind to my ears
Listen plaintive mourning
Calls across mountains
Time builds up in
Corners, crevices
Collecting dust
Of Centuries

Heart is crushed by emotion
Solitary prison, self-made
Leaving all who tender love
Standing alone oceans
Winds course their way
I am beside myself ego
A pilgrim or pensioner
Some God mysterious
Waits for closure, anon

Rabbi Schlotz Talks With Satan: -Day 50

Rabbi:

It was the emotion of things that hung over his actions, the unknown spaces of life that formed a barrier to everyday time. This impending force wanted to overwhelm him as if it was an enemy in a distant bunker foxhole waiting to shoot him if he showed himself above ground.

The desire for wanting to be understood usually centered around a woman. Men friends never could fulfill satisfaction. Women held pieces of life's puzzle that men never could imagine. Women were not only the source of man's birth but also his continuing life.

Rabbi was, once again, in love.

His need for companionship centered upon Teresa. She started out slow in his imagination. She presented herself with the promise to pray for him.

In the discussion with himself, he sent her a message:

> *This is a small crack*
> *In the wall I have built between us An*
> *internet touching of words Small but*
> *letting me hope*
> *For some future deluge*
> *When I can let out frustration*

It is my doing

I close myself
With insecurity
Give in to fear
Not wanting To
be hurt

I try my best to self-evaluate
Conduct in-door psycho-therapy
"How did you feel about that, Mr. Thomas?"

Well, I felt like a worm locked into darkness I felt
like a baby chick in a nest
No hope of growing and leaving

I turn away from the only person who really
understands me
I get what I deserve
Leave walls where they are
They are needed temporarily

Satan:
Sincerity bleeds through this.

Rabbi:
And more:
I have never met anyone like you You
are perceptive

You are kind
You give to others
You are patient
You are a high spiritual person
You are Catholic but you accept other beliefs
You know if a person has belief grounded in understanding.
I read a Chekhov short story about a man in Russia who fell in love with a married woman. The story ends with the two of them starting a relationship with each other. The story was so well written that I could not put it down. Anton Chekhov is a masterful writer. But, the story captivated me because its similarity to you and I. I have not wanted you to come up to my apartment because I do not want to put you in a precarious position since: You are an honorable person with no deceit. Coming up here would put you in jeopardy to face your family and husband with a false face.

I do not want to be the cause of that predicament.

I do know this: you and I are a fire that could start very easily.

Satan:
I will wait for you to finish before I comment.

Rabbi:
Who knew you were such a straight-up guy?

Satan: *(Thumbs his nose, laughing.)*

Rabbi Schlotz Talks With Satan: -Day 51

Rabbi:

I have an idea. I will spread the word that you have committed suicide and the world needs a new devil.

Satan:

You are whacko.

Rabbi:

Well, we will test to see who really cares for you. We will display your body in a wake prior to your burial.

Satan:

Who will you get to impersonate me in the coffin?

Rabbi:

You are **The Devil**, you can easily conjure up a person to look like **The Devil** is supposed to look, - dead.

Satan:

Maybe, I will use you as a Jewish rabbi devil.

Rabbi:

I do not care; just leave me out of the mix.
How do you want to commit suicide?

Satan:

Jump off the tallest building in the world?

Rabbi:

Kind of boring; how about suffocating in a disabled submarine?

Satan:

With a camera crew recording the last moments of my death?

Rabbi:

I think a scene where you drive off of the Grand Canyon in a Maserati with a beautiful woman unconscious next to you?

Satan:

Who will play the beautiful woman?

Rabbi:

The blessed mother.

Satan:

You are doubly whacko ...worse.

Rabbi:

We will have an after-death ceremony in St Patrick's cathedral in New York, where God appears and speaks how you had a last minute conversion back to grace.
And, how all the souls in hell are lined up alphabetically to give their confession and come back to goodness.

Satan:

I think I would prefer to be buried out of the Arch basilica of St John Lateran in Rome. It is the one main church of the Roman Catholic faith ... and, I would like the pope to officiate.

Rabbi:

We will see if the Holy Father is available.

Rabbi Schlotz Talks With Satan: Day-52

Rabbi:
Excuse me for taking your time
Only read this if you are bored
Or have nothing else to do

My ex-wife will not talk to me
After forty years of divorce
I have repeatedly tried to
make her a friend who can
carry on intelligent discourse
But, unfortunately, she has
become resistant to therapy
recovering from being found
in a Brazilian jungle clearing
by a National Geographic
team using infrared lenses

As part of my college degree
I was fortunate to be included in
the first attempts to reach her
in Psychology 101 taught by
Adam Ledbetter, the third
Who won so many awards
written on remedial methods
introducing language skills
to disadvantaged marsupial
quadruped nomadic mammals
You will probably never run into her
at the grocery store or mall where

she is always cloaked, accompanied
by inauspicious companions who
retrieve items she points to with
her gloved finger wavering

Her mannerisms have not changed
even from the county judge who
asked her to point out the man
in the courtroom who hurt her
she singled me out with horror

She disdains society
She clamors for secrecy
She has been too damaged
By my leaving her friendless
after only five years of what I
generally refer to as worst of my life

Satan:
(yawns)

Rabbi:
Waking to the immediate muffled sound of a dog barking.
Consistent barking that makes me aware of owners who are not
attending the creature.
Fledglings in a nest depend upon their parents bringing worms
or insects.
I have mixed feelings about the benefit of pets: pets who have a
natural element away from human involvement, pets whose
existence is interrupted by intervention into our households.
Aside from my having been a cat owner for years, I mistrust my
neighbors who allow their dogs to bark-and-bark while they are
away.

Satan:
What is your point?

Rabbi:
There is a fascination with linking ourselves with all elements of
evolution as a way of measurement or derivation.
I used to relish watching my cat exhibiting behavior patterns
that were indicative of natures in the wild
or natures similar to mine.
The excretory functions, the eating, stretching and sleeping
activities were so like mine as examples.
History is replete with examples of domesticated animals. Cave
dwellers always had dogs guarding their entrances in prehistoric
times. Pets develop a bond with humans whether personally
attached or by association.

Cats were sacred in ancient Egyptian society. Religions centered upon worshiping of animals existed starting 10,000 years ago. Aside from the nobility of statutes of cats, their value was great in keeping granaries free of mice. Icons or mummified cats were placed in burial sites as a way of honoring the deceased. They were placed in burial sites as part of things that the deceased would have on the other side of the veil, after death. Inanna Ishtar, queen of heaven and earth was the Goddess of love, beauty, sex, desire, fertility, war, combat, justice and political power.

She had chained lions that accompanied her in circa 4,000 BC or BCE - Before The Common Era. I am sure she had servants feeding and caring for their cleanliness. I wonder if their growling kept people awake.

Bootes, the constellation home to Arcturus: third largest star in the night sky next to Sirius or Canopus, has the depiction of a herdsman with two hunting dogs on a leash. Their names are Asterion and Chara.

Years ago, Carolyn denounced people who took walks without leashing their dogs. The dogs would bark and threaten people in their path. It was fearful to guard against being bitten.

People who leave their dogs in a closed home alone probably never consider how the dogs miss their presence and bark over and over to express their loneliness.

It is upsetting to me to have my thought stream broken by dogs barking and the sound coming through the thin walls we live within.

Is hell populated by creatures bringing torment to damned souls?

Satan:

All your questions will be answered if you sell your soul to me.

Rabbi Schlotz Talks With Satan: Day-54

Rabbi:

It will not matter one bit that blood ran through my veins for a short number of years on this planet. No one will note or care about my life.

Satan:

I feel the same, sometimes.

Rabbi:

There never will be stories written about me. No songs or ballads. I cannot even come close to your notoriety as **The Devil**.

Satan:

Take my word for it, my fame is insignificant.

Rabbi:

But, you were at the cross at Golgotha to see Jesus die.

Satan:

He was a stubborn soul that thought his crucifixion would mean something to the world. He did not reform any souls and after his death, admissions into hell increased.

Rabbi:

Sometimes I believe the futility of good and evil is meaningless.

Satan:

Yes.

Rabbi:

I will tell you what you and God and all the enduring stories mean: I think they are like a television commercial full of nonsense and lies.

Satan:

We get the customers to call in or cash in on our pitches. We are good at getting souls to hell or heaven.

Oh, and the fun part is they bring their families and kin following them right to the depths of my lovely forever fires.

Rabbi:

You will never get me and God will never get me in either hell or heaven. I will keep on trying to be spiritual in my manner of doing good and loving my neighbor.

Satan:

You are a tough soul. I could make much of you in my chambers.

Rabbi:

You go to hell.

Satan:

Like I've never heard that before ...

Rabbi:

I am not important. Life goes around and through me as if I am invisible. I am left with my small understandings of earth and the heavens.

Besides, the knowledge base that makes our histories, keeps changing and as new things are learned, we keep getting overloaded with information that we can never get a grasp upon.

I am a positive person, but not too hopeful about futures of space and time.

Satan:

You need to overcome your deep thinking. Just take things as they are and do not go too far afield. The future will work itself out without your or my interference.

Rabbi:

The fates: The symphonies of Tchaikovsky belabored the fates. Their mournful weaving melodies were his enigmatic attempt to face the inevitable course of life.

Satan:

All music has that attempt as basic search for answers.
You know, if you hook up with me, I will make you the most famous composer of all time.

Rabbi Schlotz Talks With Satan: Day-55

Rabbi:
Where heaven swings a thread
Stars sway on gossamer fern
Pendulum moon enchanted
A heart of universal pulsing

We collect magnet mystery
Feint breathing silver dust
Dazzled dumb-found eyes
Our spirits dizzied echoes

These memories lasting
Within ancient cuneiform
Strings of silent symmetry
Attached columnar rows

I beg you hear my calling
Plaintive murmur chants
Embodied in nest music
Enticing you to my soul

I am stricken by ghosts
Who build me in songs
Carried from life ingress
Catapulting us with love

Satan:
I would create an air conditioned arena in hell just for you to
read your poems. And we could sell snow cones!

Rabbi Schlotz Talks With Satan: Day-56

Rabbi:

The world is not screwed too tight.

People want to hurt other people.

Even while they are praying peacefully in a church, someone blows them up killing and wounding so many.

What kind of hatred would make someone do that?

How in the hell can a God love these type of strange people?

Satan:

I love them.

Rabbi:

You love weirdos? You are a weirdo.

Satan:

Everyone has free will to love God or love me.

Rabbi:

I think that is the nexus or central point - free will.

God should take free will away and the world would be totally peaceful with nobody doing stupid things. So what if everyone walks around like a zombie or in a trance: They will not have the will to do bad things. It sure as hell would make things a lot quieter around the earth.

Satan:

I would stop getting souls into my doors of hell.

Rabbi:

So what? How many souls do you need to make you happy?

Satan:

Just one more than heaven has.

Rabbi:

If you go fishing, you should be satisfied with one big fish.

Satan:

If you take away free will, then God will be real busy stopping everything that might even come close to evil.

First thing that would happen is the world will never need another lawyer. Never need another judge. Never need policemen. You will still need firemen.

Rabbi:

Are there fire alarms on the walls of buildings in hell?

Satan:

Not one. We just let fires rage out of control. Big fires do not even make the news in hell.   Some of my favorite fallen souls are pyromaniacs. I love them.

Rabbi:

Did your souls induce Nero to burn Rome?

Satan: *(smiling)*
Yep.

Rabbi:
The great Chicago fire?

Satan: *(With great pride)*
Yep.

Rabbi:
… all the uncontrolled forest fires?

Satan:
Not all, but enough.

Rabbi:
… the great fire of the City of Pittsburgh in 1845?

Satan:
What great memories you conjure! Yes. Everyone in hell stayed awake to watch that one go up in flames.

Rabbi:
Ben Kastle, the son of the famous steel magnate, owned restaurants and he would burn one that needed to be refurbished. He would add a couple hundred thousand to the insurance request and he would pocket the money.

Satan:
I am well aware of the damned soul Kastle and we have a special place in hell for him with a roomful of money that he has no place to spend it for eternity.

Did you know him?

Rabbi:

I was a CPA who did audits for his restaurant chains.

You know the stories of how cheap J. P. Morgan was, well Ben Kastle was the biggest miser I have ever known. He would use his credit card to get gas for his car and add a couple of bucks on the bill that he would put in his pocket.

I cannot understand how God allows these souls to steal and cheat. Why does he not strike them down with lightning?

Satan:

Fine by me.

Rabbi:

I am going to sleep and pray for rain or a flood to wipe out all the souls on earth. You may take your pick, if you please.

Rabbi Schlotz Talks With Satan: Day-57

Rabbi:

(Interlude)

Things I did not say to her at the door, last time I saw her before she died.

"Patricia, please do not compare me to your father."

"We have had thirty five years of a friendship, now coming to an end."

"Your problems with your father and your family are all yours to deal with. I feel sorry for you because you have so many issues that are so huge and you are doing your best to overcome what would have destroyed another person who did not have your inner strength."

"We have ended this day and I leave you and promise to never come into your house, as you wish. I understand less of what has happened between us than you do. I can only say that the greatest healers of all are time and patience. "

"I have loved you without sex, purely, as my spiritual adviser and friend. We both have reached a path where we now diverge."

"I will no longer be your whipping boy. But I do not disparage you for feeling that you will not have me to blame for your problems. "

"I have been here to feel the brunt of your angers and I have no doubt that you will find some other means of solving some of the problems you have with another close person."

"You have had a life so much harder than mine and others. You were abused as a child from age nine when your mother died from over drinking. Your father, an alcoholic, and step-mother, an alcoholic, beat you with a belt buckle for over eight years. You left home at age sixteen and you married a man thirty years older than you for security. You had nine years with this husband until you left the hospital with a broken hip after having your third child. No one told you what happened and you lived for fourteen years with that pain in your hip. You left that husband who never understood your pain. Your third child, at age five, was drowned and you had this sadness added to your blackened life. For fourteen years you mourned that child. And, to boot, you could never blame the daughter who took her eyes off of him at the swimming pool, and allowed him to drown. Your daughter dominated you or blackmailed you out of possessiveness. She never apologized to you for the child drowning. Her best defense was her clinging to you hoping that she would never be blamed."

"You sat at home waiting for the child to be pronounced dead for one week and the church you belonged to never attended his funeral."

"The two things you did to overcome some of you sadness, which was burrowed into you like a metal sliver that you could never extract, was to marry Lewis, who was your friend to the end. And take me on as a student and a friend for over thirty five years."

"I cannot blame you for screaming at me at the doorway tonight. I will let you because, whether we like it or know it, we have come to the end of our relationship."

"You do not know it, but you will die in a few months and you will not allow me to visit you in the hospital or attend your funeral. Your family, who hated me for being a third wheel to your marriage, will not even talk to me."

"I have only this: I could never have overcome some of the things you were faced with, and I will always remember the good years when we talked, walked, discussed all things under the sun and let me touch you with my heart."

(End of interlude)

Rabbi:
Thou art a knave, peasant, degenerate, symbol of underbellies of slithering worms, consigned to a world of darkness never ending.

Satan:
What the hell has gotten into you? You looking for a fight?

Rabbi:
No, fine sir, what, perchance, has gotten into you. For what comes through on the exterior tells a sad tale of what is inside.

Satan:
YOU presume to analyze ME? There is no talking to you when you are in a mood.

Rabbi:
Yon mountain echoes thy fury as devil of the misty fomenting hurricanes, setting loose avalanches of death:
tumbling snow descending in rivers of destruction. You are the fallen angel who begins hell over-and-over in cries of souls caught in misguided quests for light.
Truly black holes pale beside your consuming whirlpools of suction from which nothing near you escapes.

Satan: *(Beams brightly)*

Rabbi Schlotz Talks With Satan: Day-59

Rabbi:
Wake up Mr Devil.

Satan:
What is up, my friend? Have your lawyers approved my contract with you?

Rabbi:
I do not have any lawyers. I will never sign a contract with you even if your exercise gymnasium has air conditioning.

Satan:
Too bad. I am throwing in a pocket thermostat so you can control the cold air anywhere you go in my kingdom of everlasting fire.

Rabbi:
Why do you not just kneel to God and be done with your little circus-of-hell side show.

Satan:
Why don't you kneel to me? What do you want? Why did you wake me?

Rabbi:
I want to know if there are alternate realities, will heaven and hell be duplicated?

Satan:
Can't tell you.

Rabbi:
Edward Grieg's lyrical pieces of music are to die for. He is so good and listening to his music makes me wonder if he will pop up in another solar system in the many universes that exist. His music conveys the rich sounds of Norway, the embellishment of his peoples' joys and sadness with instrumentation and depth of immense symphonic melodic flavors.
If I die and have to reincarnate within another solar system, I will demand: *Jean Sibelius, Carl Nielsen, Franz Berwald, Wilhelm Stenhammer, and Joonas Kokkonen,* all bringing to my ears the wind swept frozen northern sounds of unleashed nature at its wildest.

Satan:
You really want a lot. Maybe you should just become your own God and make it all the way you want.

Rabbi:
I, certainly, would fill your spot with Chopin or Tolstoy; or maybe ... the brothers William and Henry James and their fantastic works. I will let Pierre-Auguste Renoir paint you into oblivion.

Satan:
Like I said: Do it yourself. Besides, I have a good relationship with artists like Caravaggio - *Judith beheading Holofernes*, or Hieronymos Bosch's *Garden of Earthly Delights* or maybe, Henry

Fuseli showing me as a disgusting gnome sitting atop a dead woman. I love that painting called *"The Nightmare"*

Rabbi:
I am not stupid. I know that any reality of creative goodness will need a compensating element of evil to work itself within a full circle.
So, no matter how I cut the cake, I need your hell. But, remember, your hell can never take the whole thing over. Your hell is only a balance to good and loving natures.

Satan:
Good on you for understanding.

Rabbi:
But, I'm keeping myself on the side of peace and goodness.
I will let you be and just watch you through my binoculars or my pirate telescope.

Satan:
I will send you smoke signals like the American Indians did with their blankets over a fire.

Rabbi:
Do me a favor and just call me on your cell phone.
Leave a message and I will get back to you.

Rabbi Schlotz Talks With Satan: Day-60

Rabbi:
It is hard to get personal.
You are a devil of abstraction.
You never talk about yourself or your relationships with Gods or people around you.

Satan:
What do you want to hear?

Rabbi:
You are one of the first. One angel created by God in his image at the start.

Satan:
Yes, and ...?

Rabbi:
Do you have aunts and uncles?

Satan:
Busy yourself with your aunts and uncles.

Rabbi:
I am a lonely person who has very little physical intimacy with anyone. I still love females, but for the last forty years I have not had sex with a woman or even touched one.

Satan:

So, you want a medal? Did you have sex with a man?

Rabbi:

Please do not be sarcastic. No I do not want a medal or acclaim; I am just trying my best to be spiritual.

Satan:

Remember, you are a faulted human being and not perfect.

Rabbi:

There is a woman who I have tried to avoid, but I cannot seem to get her out of my mind. She is a kind, thoughtful person and, unlike others, she really likes me. I like her also. She has a husband, a place in society with her role as an assistant to the priest in a church.
I do not want to upset things or inveigle myself in that situation.

Satan:

You either have to stay away or get closer to her. If you sign my agreement and become a disciple of **The Devil**, I will give you a different woman every night.

Rabbi:

I am not interested in those pleasures. I only want to talk to one person who is spiritual, understanding and intelligent.

Satan:

What am I ... Chopped liver? You are a lost cause to me. Go back to sleep and call me when there is something interesting.

Rabbi Schlotz Talks With Satan: Day- 61

Rabbi:
Tell me where does the money go
When movies done, end of show
Dust of dreams no more to blow
Pony is tired, sky is moving slow
Heart beats fast blood can't flow
Down below sea level so, so low

Walking back, barn gets larger
My memory is all that matters
Wind makes the straw scatter
As a sun makes me gladder
Behind tree empty bladder
Thought of her is so sadder
Shadows climb their ladder
I wait for the rain to patter
Upon tin-roofs in laughter

Satan:
You have to stop smoking funny weed, boy.
Go lie down and get the sleep you need.

Rabbi Schlotz Talks With Satan: Day-62

Rabbi:
Hey! Satan, do you live in a changing existence?

Satan:
The only thing constant in heaven or hell is change.

Rabbi:
You contradict yourself. Hell is supposed to be eternal as well as heaven.
I believe that God and **The Devil** are facing changes that will either lead to evolution or extinction.

Satan:
Let's not discuss this topic, *please.*

Rabbi:
When the truth leads to change, it is hard to face.

Psalms of the Early Buddhists, I.lvi
(Mrs. Rhuys Davids' Translation)

"Get thee away from life-lust, from conceit,
From ignorance, and from distraction's craze;
Sunder the bonds; so only shall thou come
To utter end of all. Throw off the Chain

Of birth and death-thou knowest what they mean,
So, free from craving, in this life on earth,

Thou shalt go on thy way calm and serene," The Buddha.

II. VICTORY

"But anguish crept upon me, even me,
Whereas I pondered in my little cell:
Oh my! How have I come into this evil road
Into the power of Craving have I strayed!
Brief is the span of life yet left to me;
Old age, disease, hang imminent to crush,
Now ere this body perish and dissolve,
Swift let me be; No time have I for sloth.
And contemplating, as they really are,
The aggregates of Life that come and go,
I rose and stood with mind emancipate!
For me the Buddha's words had come to pass',--------

Mittakal! a Brahmin Bhkkuhunl.
Psam's of the Early Buddhists, I. xliii
(Mrs. Rhys Davids" Translation).

What do we take from our life? A life well led with us taking
advantage of the holiest-of-holiest existence in our bodies and
souls. What do we gain from correct thinking and unblemished
ideas of love and generous attitudes?
We are, first and foremost, creations off our own thoughts,.
How lovely that we create ourselves from within the
unsanctioned spark of our own divinity. We are all and nothing
less than God within us as impervious to all outside influence.
We pray to ourselves. We chide ourselves. We reward our own
good deeds. The light inside our hearts is the original light of a

God initiated within us as the first spark of understanding and goodness.

We are all elements of physical and spiritual embodiment. We are the first cause and the first reaction to the first cause. We are a sun within a sun; A deification of all that was and all that will be forever.

Satan:
You do go on so wistfully.

Rabbi:
Get thee to thy throne of hell and hold yourself dominion over all but my soul.
You are not a devil I believe in, nor do I believe in your hell.

Satan:
You would save a lot of conjecture by signing into my service. Imagine how free your mind would be allowing me to control your fears.

Rabbi:
I would rather have freedom of fear than servitude of your indenture.

Satan:
Spoilsport!

Rabbi Schlotz Talks With Satan: Day-63

Rabbi:

Tchaikovsky Piano Concerto 3 in E flat op 75/79
We can feel the immense searching that this composer goes
through experimenting with diminuendos and descending or
ascending crescendos.
The lovely strength of Tchaikovsky's music is his powerful
expression of emotion through the orchestra and, in this case,
the piano.
We are aware of how emotion controls our experience on this
planet in this body. We know how the rich feeling we have of a
particular time or place is always kept within our hearts longer
by the feeling we have for the experience.

I have loved you deeper than a piano concerto
Lasting as a receptacle of holiness within me
I have loved you in a dizzy cyclone of music notes
Creating a vortex of fanciful sounds within my ears

Satan:

You are too romantic for me.

Rabbi:

And you are too diminutive for me.

Satan:

Aha!

Rabbi:
The whole purpose of Satanism is to reduce love down to the
outer reaches of hate.
I refuse to carry my heart past the light and into the darkness of
your blindness.

Satan:
You are the blind one. I face hate squarely. I embrace it. Rather
than succumb, I use it to my advantage.

Rabbi:
I embrace the gift of Tchaikovsky and his place above hate. He
speaks to us in the second movement Andante of Op 75
Concerto with everlasting light coming from the melody
of his heart.
If you listen carefully to this movement you will find
Rachmaninoff piano concerto number
two second movement, mirrored.
When we hear great music it attaches itself to all the music we
have ever heard. We hear Grieg opening our ears to his
Norwegian influences. We hear Sibelius shouting across the
silent expanses of Finland cold and bitter windswept extremes.

Rabbi Schlotz Talks With Satan: Day-64

Rabbi:

I want to discuss my uncle John Consiglio.

His life embodied a series of subjects that overlapped into past and future history.

John appeared to me when I was six years old. I totally fell in love with him and have clung to him or his memory to this day.

John was the sole survivor of a Patton armored division that pushed into Germany toward the end of the war. His company or unit was surrounded by the enemy which was how General Patton moved his tank units, into the heart of the fighting with no thought of back up for the protection of his men.

John had a face cut by fire. His nose was slightly crooked. His teeth set firmly into his taut jaw. His face was menacing and powerful. He had the most beautiful blue eyes. There was a determination to his nature that swept away all opposition to his will.

I want to talk about him, but before I go into my story, I will tell you that he said things that stick to my thoughts: He said about sharing his money - "You have to let the other guy eat."

Meaning that charity was his belief and it was proper to pay your bills without being cheap.

John said about a person who he described as: "What do I care about him, I have seen men far better than him die right next to me in foxholes."

John's in-laws were crooks and he suffered by working for them and not being paid. His brother-in-law stole his fishing equipment and he swore about that fervently. His second brother-in-law never paid him large wages he was owed for the bankrupt bar that John worked in,. The third brother-in-law also did not pay John wages for working in the lumber yard that also went bankrupt.

I wander. But John was a person who people could depend upon but his generous and kind nature left him cheated often. When he arrived from the war, it was three in the morning and the whole family got up to welcome him. He was drunk. He sat like a statute come alive in the living room with his duffel bag between his legs. He deliberately kept pulling things out of the bag and describing who they were for, he would throw them around the room with no care for where they landed. I remember a bottle of perfume from France, for his wife, breaking on the wall and dripping sweet perfume down to the floor. He kept taking a drink from the bottle of whiskey as he yelled and tried to keep his words straight.

It was the most amazing scene I have ever witnessed. From that moment forward, I hung onto his side ever day doing things with him for my childhood moving to growing up.

The funny thing about John was that I became his son, in my actions and my mind. The anthropologist Bronislaw Malinowski wrote how one of the major customs of the Yanamanow Indians was to allow the aunts and uncles raise the children of their kin. It kept the subjectivity of the parents at a distance as the aunts and uncles were more objective in bringing the children up.

So, John became my father and his real son never shared what I did with John. The real son became distant from his father and also died very early, denying John the benefit of his only son as a companion.

Now, John never knew the underlying current of my relationship with him since he never recognized my deep love for him. His overriding feeling was the sorrow he let rule him over the loss of his son. And his undervalue of me as his pseudo son never became prominent.

It never bothered me, since I had a life of my own without the need for his feelings. I remember distinctly on the day I mustered out of the army and I waited till all my family was done questioning me about Vietnam, late that night, I drove to Johns house where he was sitting by himself with his feet up and his first words to me were: "So, you are home. You had to figure war out for yourself."

Now you have to understand that there are two things that happen to an acolyte - they either learn no more from their object of adoration and are ready to go out on their own,. Or, they never outgrow their need for being inferior.

With John, I always felt the separation looming between us. The altar boy gives service. I helped John & Irene build their house on 2635 Chalmers. I scoured the large malls and found wood and building materials to bring home to John. I toiled with him to thread pipe and build all the rooms where he raised his daughters. I brought canned food from the grocery store in boxes that fed them free.

After Vietnam, I worked with John doing construction jobs and I imagined a partnership with him where we went out, together and made money.

Funny thing was that John did not know how to direct my enthusiasm and we found each other at odds with the work we did. He needed to feel in total control of what was going on. After a few jobs, we stopped working with each other,.

I remember the final break between us when, on a summer day, I bought beer and we took my fishing rods to the spillways in Mt Clemens. I laid the blanket out and set the beer and began to bait my hook. I noticed John struggling, and without interruption, I walked over to him and took his rod reel away from him and then I set the leader, baited the hook and handed the rod back to him ready to use. It was a pivotal moment as I cast my line out, set the rod in a stand with a bell atop to signify a catch, then lay back on the blanket and slept.. I knew instinctively that my time as John's apostle was at an end. He no longer was my God. I had outgrown him.

The world is a class of human beings who do not think of prehistoric events that have been covered over
by time and dust.

The great civilization of Atlantis lies below the sea near Florida. These peoples used sound as a means of constructing their edifices. They bypassed fossil fuels and they ended up destroying themselves, just as all other groups of people did or will do in the space of time.

We use piston driven engines and we have nuclear power enough to blow the whole planet to pieces.

The first books of our time - the Iliad and Odyssey tell of war between Greeks and Trojans.

Prior to these stories, Babylonia and Ur
destroyed themselves by war.

The Egyptians and Romans finished themselves off with their killings and tales of battles.

We have been left with the remnants of the tablets of Gilgamesh or the green tablets of Thoth warning us of our wayward bellicose natures and the inherent dangers of ego driven madness.

Our small continent of North America, pales compared to the destruction of European cities.

In America we started out with our American Revolution, our war of 1812, our Indian massacres, our civil war, Spanish American war, World war one and two, Vietnam and our involvement with oil rich countries where we subtlety and quietly kill others.

So, my uncle John came back from the war that saved the world from Hitler. He watched as America
never faced peace for very long.

Who are we and what does history mean to us?

We call ourselves Christians, Jews, Muslims; Buddhists all pronouncing love your neighbor and love your God. And all we do is kill each other.

We call ourselves honest and all we do is steal.

We believe our religions without ever questioning how each religion takes from the past without acknowledging the customs and rite we derive from.

So, John came back from war. He never went to school. He lived a good life with a wife and made accommodations to suit his needs. His son died. He had three daughters. One lives her life out not believing in God or anything spiritual. They proudly speak of their heathenism like they live isolated from all the miracles that Gods give us, yet they share those miracles with all of us. The second daughter lost her husband and follows a church religion. The third daughter was one of the few who graduated college and became a teacher, married an attorney and is wise and thoughtful.

John's wife is what I would call a Neanderthal Christian. She has become a church widow who hopes God will reward her for her faith, hope and charity. She could never discuss any other God but Jesus despite all the evidence supporting so many other Gods and wise people.

I can never fault these people, since there is space on earth and between the stars for their belief systems to exist without invading mine or yours.

If there is a God, there are many Gods. If there is an overriding belief system, that system is in flux or changing always. The only religion I find comfort in, is one of no belief systems but one of "Father forgive them, for they know not what they do."

Even I know not what I do.

Satan:
You know, I missed out on John's soul.
He slipped between the cracks.

Rabbi:
I am glad for that. He is too nice to have been captured by you.

Satan:
Well, I will make up for it with his son-in-law about to sign for everlasting atheism.

Rabbi:
You are bad.

Satan:
As long as souls want to believe in the nonexistence of God, good for them.

Rabbi:
I suppose you wish God would disappear forever?

Satan:
Stop projecting. You were discussing John ... Get on with it

Rabbi Schlotz Talks With Satan: Day-65

Rabbi:
Are you awake?

Satan:
What do you want?

Rabbi:
Someone to listen.

Satan:
It might cost you.

Rabbi:
There is no money in heaven or hell.

Satan:
We have credit cards that withstand fire.

Rabbi:
I bet.
Listen. I have been reading the Tibetan Book of the dead. It is one of the most interesting books I have ever come across.
The writer confirms so many things and goes beyond them into deep discussion.
His premise is that death and life are equal. When we live or die we make our own choices.

Upon death there is a layer of physical where male and female control the souls' choices and also there is a temporary heaven or hell that the soul can outgrow to reach above the first level.

Satan:
Once I got you, I do not care what your books say.
I have you forever.

Rabbi:
I do not think so. You are not forever with your hell fire.
Besides the cost of keeping that place hot is more than you can pay, over time.

Satan:
Do not worry about my budget, just sign these papers before I get a little impatient with you; give you pestilence and such.

Rabbi Schlotz Talks With Satan: Day-66

Rabbi:
Sun Tzu *On The Art Of War* is my latest book to read.

Satan:
Outstanding. I use that book to woo people to my furnace of hell.

Rabbi:
I suppose your favorite line is: "All warfare is based on deception"

Satan:
I never lie to a soul that is poised to enter my gates.

Rabbi:
Gates of hell. Sounds like a dime store novel.

Satan:
"When able to attack, we must seem unable; when using our forces, we must seem inactive; when we are near, we must make the enemy believe we are far away; when far away, we must make him believe we are near."
I had Jesus to myself in the desert and I got him so tired that he did not know left-from-right.

Rabbi:
I do not know about you.

Satan:

You certainly don't! General George S Patton was my buddy and I can call him up to prove he is in hell. He used Sun Tzu's book to defeat Hitler's panzer divisions.

Rabbi:

What did you use to claim Patton for hell?

Satan:

I promised him victory over any enemy he faced. He bought it. But he forgot to ask if hell had any enemies to defeat. I blinded him and captured him.

Rabbi Schlotz Talks With Satan: Day-67

Rabbi:
I had a dream.

Satan:
Let me alert the media.

Rabbi:
Apparently there is a girl. She is a student, oriental, beautiful; In the same university that a man attends as an American foreign student.

There are no names attached to the dream, only it is spring. Something about cherry blossoms imbues the air with lightness, exotic and scented to making the love between them enhanced. We all know that life is a mystery: Vacillating between breathing and impending death or encroaching decay. The foreign student is reading Henry James and is entranced by that author's magnificent depth of language. It is not the same vernacular as Hemingway - terse-and-punchy. Nor is it the intelligent way Tolstoy wrote developing character in detail.

Joseph Conrad was a Polish born novelist who displayed his aptitude in his adopted language in America. His use of words lent themselves to plot and circumstance of his captivating heroes. Charles Marlow, Lord Jim all fictitious but well developed persons that keep the reader fulfilled.

Well, our foreign student knew all these books and the language of romance in the poetry of the orient in its nature-induced beauty.

Henry James seemed to hold our student by the extravagance of language. Our student remembers one particular teacher who criticized James for too much description. But our student, of no name, favored James's books and thought of that way-of-thinking, as to how he felt toward the girl who, coincidentally, shared many of his classes.

He imagined scene after scene with her - all different - all covered in cherry blossom aroma and the faerie sense of abstract bewitching.

These things did not matter to the police official who was watching our student with mistrust.

The dream did not explain why the suspicion existed, but every action of the student seemed to add to the police official looking for a way to catch the student in falsity. The student was aware of the police official and in fear of him.

The dream, also, did not reveal to us whether there was a crime, but it was laden with that aspect of the police official's scrutiny. This dream was one that the dreamer wished would reoccur each time he slept and awoke remembering, - simply because it was a refreshing dream with a mysterious background lurking. These events of the student bewildered the police official as he stood in the empty room in the vacant building. A "For Rent" sign had a local phone number scrawled on it.

A gas fireplace protruded from the wall -lonely by itself in the room. Funny thing, there were no windows; No natural light, only the blinking neon light hanging from the dirty ceiling.

Something caught the eye of the police official. Very slight semi-circle scrapes indicated something out of place on the floor in front of the fireplace.

He tapped the wall with a resonant hollow sound, and then found a fingerprint smudge, when pressed, that caused the fireplace to swing open, revealing a hidden room.

Satan:
A hidden room? How original.

Rabbi Schlotz Talks With Satan: Day-68

Rabbi:
Music comes out of the heads of composers who hum their
melodies as they piece them into the orchestra.
The miracle of linking oboes to clarinets to violins to cello and
the boom bang lonely guys who stand with their balled up dust
mops that resonate the kettle drums and make the room afraid
of a storm approaching.
Composers are wild with batons who conduct themselves as if
they are shaving in the morning with the lather rolling off onto
their fat bellies that are indications of too much pizza and beer.
Oh! You do not like fat composers? Well, we will give you
skinny skeletons that are waiting for Halloween or some scary
movie to start with their wands calling out the wild winds of
nature's northern climates.
Give us waterfalls of forest green sliding into the hungry ocean
where dolphins wonder if whales are their parents.
Give us cliff edges of cadenzas with notes on the page jumping
skip-rope with clicking meter redundancy.
Give us life being born between the legs of screaming women
who have learned to hate sex and men for doing this to them as
Gods way of making them victim of evolution's progress. And
those asshole Johnny-jump-up bean-heads who want to take the
right away from us to have an abortion. May they all go to hell
with breach birth babies coming out of their torn uterus walls.
May the God of forgiveness who attaches himself to Rondo
Accelerando - Ritardando change into a woman who bakes
muffins in a gas oven in twelve cup containers with paper
inserted before the dough is plumped into each section. May
that God open his or her eyes to a sun coming past the barn

where the horses are whining for hay, water and for someone to ride them so they feel useful.

Hold onto the mis·e·re·re of sorrow that spins itself out like a ball of yarn in soft hues of silicone sadness. It will catch your throat like a noose that snaps as the chute is open and you float free over the crowd that has assembled to hear the dirge of your death swoop over the town as your soul escapes its lonesome heaviness within the disappointment
of all your adventures of bitterness.

Go to the cupboard and find it bare. But from the fields the slaves will echo a spiritual that will free you from cotton and soybeans coughing up money at the harvest.

Do not let this dissertation of exhausting subjects sway you from your hold on sanity. You are not insane if you can outwit the Great Horned Owl from pair calling at the dark hour from the roof tops and tree branches of the moon striated shadows that stain the crisscrossing of lace over the invisible farms and blatant cities of light and noise.

Call out to heaven to show you a slice of wisdom. Does all we learn turn itself into distaste? When we become overcome with our appetites and we no longer watch cooking shows because the cooks always assume their spouses till take them back after they have licked all the spoons and taken their aprons off.

Satan:
Was there any sanity in your family?

Rabbi Schlotz Talks With Satan: Day-69

Rabbi:
I had a lover with a face like cabbage
She traveled light with little baggage
She Spoke gentle but broke savage
"Look before you love" was her adage

She saw up close and far past her nose
She wore both men's or women's clothes
Her hardness was an exterior pose
She's soft and gentle to all she knows

Satan:
It is just the right time
For a swell rhyme

Rabbi:
Do you ever wonder if you have quirks that other people see that you do not?

Satan:
As **The Devil**, I do not need to be too self-reflective.

Rabbi:
Why the hell not?   You are one of the most recognized and notorious souls that has ever existed.   You challenge God and because of you, hell comes into prominence.

Satan:

Remember, I am evil and you do not have to work too hard to be so. All things that exist always start out, kind-of, nice. So, for someone like me, it is simply easy to speak out against good. Good exists and evil comes from it.

If good did not exist, I would be in trouble.

Rabbi:

That makes sense, but do you have aspects of personality that you have never become aware as an objective person?

It is simple to be evil and subjective because nothing there changes.

But, to be evil or **The Devil**, are there parts of you that you never considered? Like, for instance: If you are standing in line at Starbucks, waiting to get a cup of latte with fresh cream heated to just the right temperature, and some one behind you says: "It is a hot day." Do you suddenly realize that you are the reason things are so hot because your hell-fire surrounds you?

Satan:

You are such a wacko. Your problem, (If you are considering things that you are not aware of) is that you analyze too much. You delve into things so deeply that reality gets confused by all your ramblings.

Rabbi:

Well, maybe you forget that I am a human being and I am imperfect. So, when people point things out to me, I listen very carefully.

Satan:

If someone tells me that my zipper is open, I do not even care. I just tell them to go to hell.

Rabbi:

You are wacko. If you are **The Devil**, with an image to uphold, you better zip up your pants.

Satan:

Why do I have to worry about my genitals, when I have a tremendous tail hanging out that I can whack them with?

Your poem, that you started today's session with, postulates a person or lady who is blind and cannot even pick the right clothes.

Maybe, I am blind, but I have power and you, Mr. Rabbi, better stay out of my way or I might just convince you to sign these papers and let me take possession of your soul.

Rabbi Schlotz Talks With Satan: Day-70

Rabbi:
I have thoughts.   Are you up to listening?

Satan:
I suppose, Go for it.

Rabbi:
America has a buffoon for a president. He is like a rich child who thinks his money allows him to overstep the bounds of courtesy. He has no regard for loving his neighbor as he would like to be loved.

Satan:
I, the holder of all evil in the universe, agree with you. I am very nice to the souls that I situate in hell.

Rabbi:
Well, your hell is a whole other ball game. But for now this president is opening the door for other followers to behave badly.
And, the souls that follow this president are the bungling idiots who think that the government has the right to control a woman's right to abort.
Not one of those souls would take a baby to raise if they had to. Not one of those souls consider that the soul does not enter the embryo until after it is born and the soul decides if it is going to stay in the embryo right after entering. The soul may decide that the goals of using that embryo may have changed and there

is no use to stay with that embryo, which is the only cause of crib deaths.

Also, none of those stupid people consider the fact that population is increasing too fast to feed all the souls on earth.

Also, none of those stupid people consider the fact that, whether or not abortion is legal, that over twenty million women abort their babies legally out of choice if they want to. Another twenty million have illegal abortions. That is a constant number around the world - fifty million abortions and half of them take place under conditions of poor medical assistance. Therefore, over one half of the abortions result in medical problems.

We treat our women like they are animals who have to tend for themselves when it comes to trying to get rid of a baby that they cannot feed or do not want mentally.

This president enjoys playing God with the Supreme Court and societies attempt to override the right a woman has to control her own body.

Satan:
There are more people for me to get into hell; so, leave them alone. I don't go poaching your customers.

Rabbi:
A human health problem has nothing to do with your evil designs.

Satan:
I have told you that I am not evil. I simply take the cue from all the souls who stray from the path of goodness and justice.

Rabbi:

Have you ever considered reconciling your differences with God and simply burning your hell to the ground?

Satan:

And if the universe is to be balanced,
who will supply the evil portion?

Rabbi:

I think you and God love the power each of you have over souls. God is as bad as you with trying to convert souls to good over evil. In fact, I hate to go to church because the ministers all talk about is evil and avoiding it.
All you talk about is evil and how to cherish it.
Let me tell you that whether a supreme court rules against abortions, women will have their abortions regardless. From ancient times till now, women have found ways to abort; and population will become too large to sustain its growth. People will die from overpopulation. The population cannot sustain itself.

Rabbi Schlotz Talks With Satan: Day-71

Rabbi:
When I talk to you, I feel that you do not face the truth about yourself and reality.

Satan:
And you do? Why should I? ... I am **The Devil**.
I am the second only to God.
I am probably more truthful than God.

Rabbi:
How so?

Satan:
I do not beat around the bush with salvation and how good or bad you have been. When I get your soul, it is all bad - no degrees. Souls that reach me are 100% bad as bad can be.
In other words, the fire in my hell is same for all the souls here.
One soul cannot complain that it is a little cooler on the west end of hell.

Rabbi:
What I mean by the truth is that you and God have expiration dates just like all souls without exception. God dies eventually.
God sleeps all the time. You die eventually and sleep a lot.
All the great writings about life and its meaning, affirm that all souls die and have an existence on the other side of the veil, just as you and God have.

Satan:
How can you be so sure of yourself? Do you really think if it is written it must be true?

Rabbi:
That's the whole point, I am not sure but I read a hell of lot more things than you do. You smirk and act evil, but you never introduce discussion with me about what you read or think about,.

Satan:
How dare you!!! I am Satan and I know everything...............

Rabbi:
The hell you do. You do not know everything.
Let me prove it to you: You are forbidden from viewing parts of all souls that exist. Every soul has an area of privacy that neither you nor God can look into.
Our special private thoughts and actions are ours only.
The rule is that as long as we do not hurt others, we are allowed to be hidden when we want.

Satan:
You are very smart. I could sure use you in hell.

Rabbi:
Forget it. You will never get your hands on me.

Satan:
Famous last words. If you change your mind, I will be ready for you.

Rabbi:

You are avoiding the main theme of this discussion: Number 71.
The main issue is that you and God will die out someday and
there is nothing you can do about it.

In fact, it should comfort you and God that you are made to the
image and likeness of us humans - Just as we are made to the
image and likeness of you and God.

Satan:

Neither God nor I are Jews..

Rabbi:

Oh! So you do not like Jews?

Satan:

You Jews are all crybabies. I do not need to tell you that you live
in an isolated delusion that the Messiah has not arrived.

Jesus, Mohammad, Confucius, and Buddha all were Messiahs.

Rabbi:

Some of my Jews are a little stubborn. I accept all the Messiahs
you mention and there are a lot more, my friend. I also eat pork
and I bow to the east or whatever direction suits me.

We are veering from my supposition that all souls, without
exception, have circular existences. When the soul has reached
the end of its temporary learning lessons, it must die and start
all over again.

You should feel good about that, because you will have another
chance to not deny God in another existence, or feel that you
are better than him. In fact, in another time and place, God will
kneel to you without any rancor.

And, in another time and place there will be no need for a hell.

Satan:
Your discussions always end up with me starting over.

Rabbi:
What do you want? Do you want to hear people cry for water forever? It must get a little tiresome to listen to the same story over and over. And, you have to listen to the same denial of wrongdoing by all the guilty souls in hell. Very few people face the truth that they are the cause of their own situations. Even you and God have that problem.

Satan:
I am tired of talking to you.

Rabbi:
I am tired of trying to reason with you.

Satan:
You call that reason? Maybe we need a referee?

Rabbi:
Yea, with a yarmulke and a whistle.

Rabbi Schlotz Talks With Satan: Day-72

Rabbi:

You ask, how can you get along without her?

Do I get lonely?

I answer: I pretend that she is dead.

The response to most questions of this nature is to think of things as being unavailable, like everything you love is gone and unreachable by touch or thought.

I have always considered love and enjoyment as fleeting. It is much better to think of things as they will be, gone so soon.

I am not strong enough to re-create Debussy nocturnes out of my imagination without the recording or sheet music or instruments. I do not have the depth of creativity to even begin a Beethoven symphony or concerto, like the beginning of the triple concerto or the two great crashing cords of the whole orchestra at the onset of symphony three that starts with a flurry of excitement never heard before in all of existence.

She is dead, to me.

Beethoven is dead to me.

Edward Grieg is dead to me.

You, **The Devil**, are dead to me.

I love God. I love you before you fell, and now I pray for all of you, but you are dead to me where I cannot touch you,

Do you understand?

The taste of an orange is gone forever. I cannot slice the air and create the aroma of fruit.

She is absent from my reach. I no longer can feel her tongue in my mouth as she liked to kiss like I was a slice of lemon to her. She drank my saliva. She reached into my mouth like a hungry lizard or fledgling bird.

But, she is bygone; a thing of the distant memory that dissolves with time like water goes away in the desert morning. No more dew lays upon the cactus leaf. No more moisture upon my lips of passion.

It is not with sorrow that I think of her. Why cry over the joy gone? When dwelling on the past overtakes dwelling on the present, it is an impediment to truth. Truth can only be perceived when we are at our full attention. Thinking about the past blocks our ch-okras.

There is heaviness to thinking too much about things of the past. When that heaviness burdens us, we cannot let our heart to be open. Placing her in least-important is a healthier way to live. We can drown in our tears of regret.

"Do not cry for me Argentina." should be our attitude.

There are only two things to cry for: One, the injustice of inhumanity and two, the injustice of my ignorance.

I cannot control behavior of others. I cannot control my ignorance. My ignorance is my attempt to find out what life is all about by trial-and-error.

That is what love was with her: Attempts to try happiness for a while and then: Puff!, she is gone. Love is gone. Why even begin to regret. Love is a finite endeavor of ineptitude. Life is an infinite burden of failures turned into seasoning on our main meal of experience.

Satan:
You are attempting to expand your thoughts? How's that working for you?

Rabbi Schlotz Talks With Satan: Day-73

Rabbi:
Why do I have to start every conversation with you?

Satan:
I don't summon you, you summon me. Besides, you have more to say.

Rabbi:
I am feeling lonely. We have a president in America that is like the beginnings of Hitler.
We have so many things at our disposal in the way of information that we sometimes get lost with the topics and subjects that we can chose from.

Satan:
It has been that way since all time. Objective thought is a waste of time. It gets bogged down in the minutia of detail and often misses the more important factor of: how does it support survival?

Rabbi:
Don't you get overload?

Satan:
I have only one thing to worry about: Damned souls.

Rabbi:
I often turn to classical music to relieve my tedium.

Satan:

Good choice. *Night On Bald Mountain* or maybe *Dr. Faustus*?
By the way: Quit yawning while you're talking to me. If you are tired get some rest.

Rabbi:

I am listening to Goetz Piano Concerto in B flat Opus 18 with Hamish Milne and the BBC Scottish Symphony Orchestra Michal Dworzynski conducting.
B flat major is one of my favorite keys,.
Yes, I am tired. Thank you for listening to me. God pays no attention to me. He is so busy. You just seem to have nothing to do.

Satan:

Go to hell, bat eyes! I am busy, too.

Rabbi:

Something empty and scary sets inside my heart. Even though my life is peaceful, there is always something, seemingly missing.

Satan:

I told you. It has been like that for all of time for all souls. Here is a hint: Place very little importance on those occasional doorways to depression. Give them small significance and get on with your life. Remember what someone said: *"Learn something new and your depression will go away."*
Also remember that there is a difference between normal sadness and depression. Do I need to go into that for you?

Rabbi:

No. And thank you. Sometimes you are a gentleman.

Satan:

You keep that to yourself!

Rabbi Schlotz Talks With Satan: Day-74

Rabbi:

When I go to my typewriter, all the surrounding conditions of comfort have been arranged; Music chosen tonight is Eduard Grieg; Lights are dimmed; Tea is brewing; Medications taken; Clothing chosen and overhead fans are turning silently stirring slight breezes making me feel like I

am outdoors breathing easily.

I have two thoughts: one: The physical life and all actions attuned to it. two; The ephemeral emotion behind it..

Satan, do you think like that?

Satan:

God, no! You are a hard person to read. Your thoughts are always out of the ordinary and I have to pay attention to understand you.

In answer to your question: Yes my incidental surroundings are a platform from which I can step back from and think about them.

It is the old story of getting outside of yourself to see yourself as clearly as possible.

Rabbi:

The worth of my life in balance is how I feel good about myself. I try to see if I am doing the right things and mainly, pleasing others as well as pleasing myself.

I feel love for those close to me and those away from me, all of whom were or are a part of my memory: My imagination of being liked by my son, sisters, work partner and "bump-into" people that I come into contact with.

I remember a lady in the elevators in Detroit telling me that I was a bright spot in her life, just by her running into me riding the elevators. There were manned elevators and each morning I would greet the man or woman sitting on the stool turning the handle to open or close the door and engage the lift mechanism. Of course, I am aware of how people react to me. I always look for good reactions. I never met that woman, but it pleased me that she liked the poetry I would read from memory while all the people in the elevator tried to remain silent
till their floor was reached.

Now, there is a prominent aspect of me that: I like to get people to come out of their shells and come alive when I am near them. Sometimes the reaction is negative for those who like to be left alone to their privacy.

I do know this: You can never know what a person is thinking unless you break their seclusion and force them to speak.

Now, remember, I am not a very wise person but I am trying to live my life of joys and sorrows, pains and comforts within the fact that I am going to die and start over with another life.

I read the Tibetan book of the dead, the Thoth emerald tablets, the Egyptian book of the dead, the Bible, the Koran, and all the ancient and current writings that postulate a level of existence above the life-and-death one of reincarnation. I read how souls, even God and **The Devil**, must sleep a lot to refresh their consciousness.

But, taking the elevator to go to work, is all I can do to be myself. I cannot be anything else but what I am.

Satan:
No one sane expects more from you.

Rabbi:

I will tell you this: When the emotion of life overtakes the events of life, then I feel the most alive. I love when music, words, art awakens me to new emotions of awareness.
Do you feel the same way?

Satan:

I kind-of stay above all that emotion and just like to scare the hell out of souls to get them into my domain.

Rabbi:

Why do you even bother with me? I am never going to be one of your damned disciples.

Satan:

Famous last words! You are interesting ...
and just leave it at that.

Rabbi Schlotz Talks With Satan: Day-75

Rabbi:
I deserve
Nothing less than safety
I am anointed
With sanctimony
Grace falls over me
In apple orchards of sluices
Do not envy my robe of riches
Solomon pales
Moses speaks through me
Lazarus talks of me incessantly
Job cries my name at gates of the city
Imploring God his jealousy sway heaven

Below ocean secrecy
I speak aloud all mysteries
As great sea storms roil measures
Towers, higher than mountains swell
beyond the eye of belief

Satan:
Were that it was as you speak it!

Rabbi:
I sleep
I wake
All light bundled in therapies
Washes my heart of delusions
Cover me over in lace
Guild me in fragrances

Allow morning dew
Dry Upon places of passions
Collected silicone sadness
Vibrates echoes riveting

Teutonic plates sewn rifts
Those divisions inseparable
Form a mosaic about my soul

Rabbi Schlotz Talks With Satan

Rabbi Schlotz Talks With Satan: Day-76

Rabbi:
I blame eventualities,
covered over by supposition's promising impossibilities.
I blame you, Mr Devil,
and you do not even deserve your name capitalized.

Satan:
I can promise you eternal bliss.

Rabbi:
At the expense of loss of my eternal soul.

Satan:
Think of the possibilities of being third in line behind God and
me.

Rabbi:
I simply prefer to be two hundred fifty zillion in line but be free.
I am free to be despondent or delirious. I prefer to be ignorant
or investigative. But still totally free of your or God's will.

Satan:
You are a fool to give up so much. Tell you what I will do. I will
give you a free one day pass for hell and you can roam about my
garden of fire ravaged flowers that bloom forever in blood red
brilliance or sunrises that never set.
I will give you freedom from guilt or doubt.
Think about the possibility of absence of possibilities.
Think about happy endings for all of remaining time.

Look, you postulate that God and I will someday die or be forgotten by artificial intelligence that will create their own God on some external hard drive on some unknown master computer that is powered by the energy of all the suns in the universes.

I will tell you this: You are the most intelligent being I have ever come across, and you deserve the place of your own star group.

Rabbi:
I do not even have to think about it.
Your promises are paper thin.
Your rewards expire.
Your heart has a membrane covering over all the darkness that would black out all of time forever.
You are a sinkhole of madness and all I can do is pray for you.

Satan:
Ha! Pray for **The Devil**. I love it.
I will pray for you, Mr. Rabbi Schlotz.
I will pray that you submit to your expectant Messiah, being me.

Rabbi Schlotz Talks With Satan: Day-77

Rabbi:
I do not have the level of spiritualism or depth of fortitude to be much more than a scared human being who gets old and dies. You, Mr Devil and all the Gods, angels and souls who left us with their bravery and histories that give me examples to which heights I will never rise.

The World War II was a debacle of insanity where Hitler and the world stepped past the Iron Age and Medieval Age and refined the Industrial Age in spectacles of killing with tanks, bombs and machinery that outstripped all of history's achievements.

We have never seen the likes of terrifying interactions between human beings, ever on the earth, as in whole cities being burnt to the ground with aerial bombing. Hamburg, Aachen, Berlin all destroyed to the ground. The two warships of Hitler: Bismarck and the Tirpitz both sunk with all their thousands of sailors entombed within the steel hulks below the ocean.

When I read or learn of these things as to how over one hundred fifty thousand men dying in a few weeks along the Siegfried line of defenses that Hitler had built with entrenchments to protect Germany's Western Defenses. I become ill and upset that such things can exist in my peaceful world.

Satan:
(smiles)

Rabbi Schlotz Talks With Satan: Day-78

Rabbi:
Mister **Satan:**

These series of essays talking with you is coming to an end and will be published, soon.
If there is anything you want to tell the souls who still exist or will always exist in the "spacious present", which consists of past, present and future, then please say it now or forever hold your peace.

Satan:
I have many ways of getting my message of eternal damnation out to the public.

Rabbi:
I am sure you do, but not with so much intimacy and through me personally.

Satan:
There's the problem. You think **you** are so important.

Rabbi:
I will be glad when the Artificial Intelligence community gets rid of you and God and all the belief systems that may have held society together in the past, but are no longer the answers to eternal enigmas.

Satan:

We will always be forever.

Rabbi:

Yes, but soon to be relegated to minor importance.

Let me tell you something. Gods have come-and-gone.

Just as earth,-air,-fire,-water, all change in time, so do all eternal beliefs change forever.

All the arrogance of the innocent eventually becomes the awareness of the wise.

The waters of understanding flow along both banks of the river's edge.

Satan:

Your poetics will also always turn to blabber.

Rabbi:

Enough! I would venture to say that you have learned little from me. But, I have been pleased to have met you.

I read all I can get my hands on. I listen to all formulas and protestations of truth and I make my own mind up about how things work.

Little grains of sand grow into mountains of my heart.

I have the confidence that my moons of mistrials will become moons of awareness as I grow with quietness and wisdom.

Neither Gods of promise, nor devils of destruction can influence me.

Satan:

I will scare you with a flashlight when you least expect, and the darkness will cover you.

Rabbi Schlotz Talks With Satan: Day-79

Rabbi:

In swaddling rags
awaking to wonders
cast out of molds
dried of after-birth
smooth sun-stretched
laughter of missionaries
bursting from monasteries
echoing across eternities

I am live-and-let-die
by sylvan streams
discolored dreams
lateral infestation
literally unrestrained
by madness of free will
divided within various
similarities of genetics

there is hope in signals
awaiting a fusion of rainbows
a bleeding of fruited dreams

remarkable symmetries
of pyramids pointed to stars
where we all are awaiting
dawns of destitution
flutes of forbidden sorrows

let out of ourselves
an enervation of guilt
empty test tubes
poured forth

the last breath of science
evaporated innocence
awaiting, awaiting,
your love

Rabbi:
I have a sister who believes **The Devil** controls her.

Satan:
Yes, I know her well.

Rabbi:
She is like most of your believers, who have little education and whose fears are greater than their moral strength or their self-confidence.

Satan:
So?

Rabbi:
You have the upper hand with weak souls. Your job is made easier when their dark rooms leave them closed in.
I was rather surprised when my sister explained her daughter's drug addition to **The Devil**'s trap. I knew that her daughter was not a strong person and had only herself to blame for her addiction.
I think that my sister whitewashed her daughter's faults belonging to some other force because then she did not have to place blame on the child. In fact, the-*'devil-to-blame'* is a perfect excuse to avoid accountability.

Satan:
I get that a lot. But, if it means that I get another damn soul for my dominion, then let it be.

Rabbi Schlotz Talks With Satan: Day-81

Rabbi:

Prithee, thee fairest moon of dreams, casting shadows willy-nilly, as if thy rich beams were wont to waste themselves upon unworthy darkness.

Doth thy heart await such embraces as would light be jealous, or oft night strip away the semblances of sorrow and lay open doorways of desires to feast upon?

Satan:

You have read too much Shakespeare.

Rabbi:

Upon my knees bent to lords invisible.

Upon my folded hands in prayer, I do offer thee much penance.

Satan:

More penance is more than repentance. Give thyself over to hell's fires to cleanse thyself of the bark of sin.

Rabbi:

It is upon my soul that birds find their nest or ancient whales rest within chambers of secret ocean caves.

It is within the core of hurricanes bestirred of menace that I shake my fingers thus in retribution. Fall before the forest speaking of evils beneath the crags of twisted roots.

Ere, beneath faerie mushroom awnings do little people dance in drunkenness to sounds of merriment closing out all dangers of citizens of closure. It is thus that beneath the leaf-and-twig where quiet slips of streams carry their world downstream to oceans hungry mouths.

Satan:

You are just wacko, a verbose whacko. I do not know what to make of you.

Rabbi Schlotz Talks With Satan: Day-82

Rabbi:

While **The Devil** sleeps, I roam silent streets in moccasins and keep to the dim lit path in stealth.

Please join me in my solitude.

My thoughts follow me as slanted shadows from what little light seeps through the stars and moonless grey clouds.

We have but little time before dawn interrupts us.

I pray for my son, my gentle son who makes his mark upon the world with light impression. He is not married and I wonder that his quiet nature has kept him happy with very little complaining. I do not believe he is gay. Nor is he interested in women. My son is like a priest who is comfortable with himself.

I think about all the many experiences I have had compared to his empty slate of ventures. I give him my love and wish the best for him.

I pray for my daughter who is twice married and with three children, she has accomplished much as a hairdresser getting her college degree and becoming a teacher. She is an enigmatic person with smiles for everyone and a sense of wonder at the world. She is like her mother and takes from the world more than she gives.

I pray for her mother who is uneducated and lives with much acrimony and regret. I pray that she may get over the past and find a future of better thoughts.

I pray for my partner in business who is half my age but twice smarter than me. She has created lovely children - three from a mixed marriage. She has finished her college and passed the exams to be a CPA. She is a giving person who upholds charity and kindness to all she meets.

I pray for you as you bump into me in the shopping aisles. I give you room and let you pass me on the street. I forgive you for being impatient and wanting to get one car length ahead of me. I watch carefully before choosing the check-out aisle, so that I do not make you feel I rushed to get ahead of you. I give you my love as I watch your restless feet and hands moving as if it will help you finish faster so that you can get home, unpack your groceries and sit in your easy chair to listen to the news before you get up and prepare dinner. I see you through the window of this suspended night and watch you staring out into the night letting the atmosphere of loneliness move against your self-consciousness.

I walk with your footsteps in unison with mine. I sense your breathing and let you walk a pace ahead of me. I love your faulted human nature because we both share an incomplete spirituality; ...

but we try our best.

Rabbi Schlotz Talks With Satan: Day-83

Rabbi:
The absence of sorrow
Own nothing to borrow
Life so full, no tomorrow
Happiness we all allow
Words spoken, no vowel

A world with no sorrow to rip our hearts into sadness.
To give ourselves over to both ceremony and the blues
We have no choice but to feel emotion from love
But deep in our souls we hate what we cannot control
Love is a cheap way of taking the edge off of delusions
We transfer our doubts into the care of another person
Who pretends to understand what we never can know

Here is a life with no sorrow when we overcome feeling
When we accept misery, become accustomed to figments
In freedom from lies we learn the real truth of enigmas
We find solace within our hearts in place of doubts
Situate yourself in between all differences resolved
Let this be your dogmas there are no deliberations
There is a calling forth of quandaries of fixations
We are small people struggling with huge thoughts
Our habits keep us from letting in mysteries of light

Satan:
Sometimes you write way over my head, or it's gibberish.

Rabbi:

You, second only to God, cannot understand simplicities

Satan:

Yep! Or inanities.

Rabbi:

I write from my heart
You hear only misgivings
The God and devil are too fixed within limits
There are no limits where there is a distancing of sorrow,
To feel things we love we must feel the attached sorrow.

From beauty comes the disorder of ugliness
Along alleys strewn with detritus we look for gold
I can only hope that what we learn accidentally
We can place into our experience purposefully

We hope for loss of sorrow, but still feel sadness
We hope for clarity within the fog of our limits

Satan:

In my private moments, I hope for a God of understanding
Because when I listen to you, I find so much I do not understand

Kahlil Gibran On Love:

*When love beckons to you, follow him, though his ways
are hard and steep. And when his wings enfold you, yield
to him, though the sword hidden among his pinions may
wound you. And when he speaks to you believe in him,*

though his voice may shatter your dreams as the North Wind lays waste the garden. For even as love crowns you so shall he crucify you. Even as he is for your growth so is he for your pruning. Even as he ascends to your height and caresses your tenderest branches that quiver in the sun, so shall he descend to your roots and shake them in their clinging to the earth.

Like sheaves of corn he gathers you unto himself. He threshes you to make you naked. He sifts you to free you from your husks. He grinds you to whiteness. He kneads you until you are pliant; and then he assigns you to his sacred fire, that you may become sacred bread for God's sacred feast.

All these things shall love do unto you that you may know the secrets of your heart, and in that knowledge become a fragment of Life's heart.

But if in your fear you would seek only love's peace and love's pleasure, Then it is better for you that you cover your nakedness and pass out of love's threshing-floor into the seasonless world where you shall laugh, but not all of your laughter, and weep, but not all of your tears.

Love gives naught but itself and takes naught but from itself. Love possesses not nor would it be possessed, for love is sufficient unto love.

When you love you should not say, "God is in my heart," but rather, "I am in the heart of God. And think not you can direct the course of love, for love, if it finds you worthy, directs your course. Love has no other desire but to fulfill itself. But if you love and must needs have desires, let these be your desires:

-To melt and be like a running brook that sings its melody to the night.

- To know the pain of too much tenderness.

-To be wounded by your own understanding of love; And to bleed willingly and joyfully.

-To wake at dawn with a winged heart and give thanks for another day of loving;

- To rest at the noon hour and meditate love's ecstasy.

- To return home at eventide with gratitude;

- And then to sleep with a prayer for the beloved in your heart and a song of praise upon your lips.

Rabbi Schlotz Talks With Satan: Day-84

Rabbi:

Color me dark
My inner being is not too well lit
I am, like you, confounded by life
Which keeps me shaded from God's light

I have watched the stars swing around the sun
Seen the white moon attempting to hid itself from praise
I feel much like Schubert's D major first symphony where he
reaches toward Beethoven with much success. He is just sixteen
years old and can open his heart for us, real wide.

Color me grey for I have very little to say
I can write you of love and promise
I can stand behind the curtain
I can hide from your praise
Like Franz Schubert, I hide

The fresh sounds of Schubert
Are like a new way of hearing
The symphony gives us a higher structure
Into which the orchestra stands above all

When composers write for the symphony, they need to raise
themselves way above the concerto or other forms

When I tell you I am dark, I mean that I can only write below the
symphony of words. I cannot give you Tolstoy or Shakespeare.

Michael Thomas 233

Satan:

You are self-effaced. You always take a lower stance

Rabbi:

I wish I could rise up past my idea of who I am.

Satan:

Shakes his head and clicks his tongue.

Rabbi Schlotz Talks With Satan: Day-85

Rabbi:

It's the sadness of salvation
Sorrow of damnation
Devil and God

Spring is here
Summer is gone

We blink to changes
Forgetting what was
Feeling only what is

So soon we love
It builds upon us
To be kind to one another
Flowers bring the love

Earth is turning away in the west / forward in the east
Little strings of solitude
Leave a taste of silence

Satan:
You will forget all you know.

Rabbi:
I turn toward the unknown
With hope in my eyes

I am the leftover treasures of discovery
Sifting through my horde
I disdain the feel of gold

I avoid all desire
I live in the spacious present

Rabbi Schlotz Talks With Satan: Day-86

Rabbi:
Always first to speak
Often the fool
My life of caution
Keeps me out of trouble
But, I dare to enter the fray
And, thus, I miss much experience
With no regret, since I cannot feel misgivings for what I avoid
One thing is for certain: neither God nor **The Devil** can count on
me being one of their adherents

Satan:
You **are** a lot of trouble
I offer you an eternity of pleasure

Rabbi:
The kind of pleasure that would keep me up all night
Because one ounce of your pleasure weighs more than pounds
of anchor keeping my soul submerged forever
I am buoyant with grace and free floating through the stars

Those souls who succumb to your promises
Can only dream of the freedom that I possess

Satan:
I can give you the fame of having your name in lights

Rabbi:
The blessing of obscurity pleases me

Michael Thomas 237

Satan:

Think of the adulation that your recognition will shower upon you

Rabbi:

Tell me, Mr Satan, you are one of the most famous figures in all of history. Does that please you?

Satan:

I am not a good example as evidence for you signing onto my agreement. We are not the same in any manner. I bristle at the thought.

Rabbi:

Yea, because you cannot back up what you promise
And, by the way, God cannot back up what he promises also
There is no such thing as eternal damnation or eternal happiness
Somewhere along the line of eternity, there is the cold fact that there is only self-satisfaction with one's place on the ladder going up or the stairs going down.
Let me give you an example: When Odysseus finally got home, he had to fight another war getting rid of the suitors who besieged his wife, Penelope.
And, years later, Calypso sends post cards to Odysseus telling how she misses him. He tried so hard to forget the joy of her bed compared to Penelope, who spent her days knitting and avoiding his fumbled love making and rough warrior character

Satan:
You don't know half of the story. You assume so much fabrication

Rabbi:
Refute it. Give me your side of the story
After you doubted God, look at what you have: All existence with damned souls who shout their regrets for always.

Satan:
Again, you make up your idea of what existence is, and then, like a megalomaniac, you **believe** it.

Rabbi:
Well, Mr Webster got the best of **The Devil** and you have never gone back to New Hampshire, as the story goes ...

Satan:
Mr Webster was an eloquent speaker and brilliant mind. There are, fortunately, very, very few Daniel Websters.
But, you do not have some skill as an orator

Rabbi:
Tell me, does Doctor Faustus finally win out over you?

Satan:
Keep reading ...

Rabbi Schlotz Talks With Satan: Day-87

Rabbi:

I am feeling as good as I need to feel.

I am not perfect.

I am not totally imperfect.

I think that we all harbor a sense of dread, but we never let that feeling get the upper hand, unless we have a degraded self-image.

We do not need to be overwhelmed by joy ... In fact; it is healthy to keep our ego sublimated.

People who hide behind a false sense of happiness are only fooling themselves. When an actual negative event occurs those people do not have the tools to deal with impairments.

I once read that the sane person keeps both sides of the spectrum in balance - feeling good and feeling wary.

Satan:

Sometimes you *overthink* things.

Rabbi:

Do not say that. My family always cautions me to not think too much.

I have learned that I never can think too much.

The more I think, the better off I am.

Satan:

(With surprise.) I believe you are serious!

Rabbi Schlotz Talks With Satan: Day-88

Rabbi:
Achtung!!
We have taken up positions surrounding hell.
We posted notices, throughout the city, informing those
interested in repatriation,
to be allowed to leave in an orderly fashion.
All will be given cake and coffee, while they wait.

Satan:
Devil's food cake, I should hope?

Rabbi:
And, fudge brownies.
It is unfortunate, but you are under house arrest. It will do you
no good to attempt escaping.

Satan:
Another of your spurious fantasies?

Rabbi:
Your little bit of heaven - in hell, is over.

Satan:
(Playing along) Your little ploy has caused my shares of stock to
plummet into bankruptcy mode. They are worthless. Whatever
shall I do?

Rabbi:

Well, you will have Long Term Capital Losses for eternity, if you want to wait to use them.

Rabbi Schlotz Talks With Satan: Day-89

Rabbi:
My Devil:

I have come to liking you.   I do not think you care one iota for evil. You simply go along with the desecrated souls that castigate themselves as evil.
Those souls feel the need for feeling despicable about themselves.
I believe that your pride will diminish, and if you could find a way to "bend-the-knee" to God you would.

Satan:
Maybe; but that sounds like a first-grader attempting to explain relativity to me.

Rabbi:
I have been formulating an idea about life.
My conclusion is that the past is best left alone.
Of all the experiences I have had, I do not want to go back.
The past has been tested on the physical plane and going back is a waste of time. The present and future are more exciting since they are yet to be tested and experienced.

Satan:
That is very astute of you. There is little reward in repeating failures.

Rabbi:

When you think about it, reincarnation is the principal cycle on the earth plane. We start each life independent of all previous lives.

Surely, we keep all past experience held tight within our genetic coding and that past is "innately" used subconsciously, when we need it.

I will tell you a story. I had a spiritual adviser who once told me that one of my lifetimes was John Milton. I am not aware of that life. But I am, like Milton, a writer and my preoccupation of reconciling Christianity with Buddhism, Mohammedanism, and all other religions, was a large focus of Milton's writing of "Paradise Lost"

As I went through college, I held a rather low opinion of Milton, since his concern for spirits was mundane to me.

In one particular class, I spoke out to denounce Milton for being boring.

In my heart, I felt, somewhat, like I was denouncing myself without really knowing why.

Milton was a rather modern writer. His works can be placed between Aeneas and the more current writers or poets like Chaucer, T. S. Eliot, or Shakespeare.

Satan:

You have surpassed the beliefs of Milton, for what that's worth, in your current writings. But, now you are like a first-grader attempting to explain quantum mechanics.

Rabbi:

I want to add this also. I would never want to go back to my divorced marriage. That situation ended forty five years ago and we were different people back then.

I do not want to go back to any of the many jobs I once held.

I do not want to ever go back to the houses I have lived in. Those living situations were once fixed within the physical and now they are fixed within the memory vogue. They now exist only as thought.

I say this because I have made myself very comfortable in my house and any consideration to move has been eliminated. I do not want a new house because I am not done with this home and all the comforts I have.

I will know with it is time to leave and step outside this situation. But, not yet.

D H Lawrence writes of his living situation in his books. He tells of how the emotion of his apartment has worn off and he is anxious to move to new lodgings.

Satan:

I have the best lodgings imaginable waiting for you. Very cheap! Just sign here.

Rabbi:

Similarly, you will also know when to leave your hell and move forward.

Rabbi Schlotz Talks With Satan: Day-90

Rabbi:
Around thy head let bells ring
From mouths a song to sing
Life's short, love's everything
Heart's a feather time swings

Satan:
Blah. Give me a black soul
To night's darkness bring
Hellishness, hate's a thing
Angels fear bleakness

Rabbi:
Tie thy heart to feathers
Lift thine eyes to heaven

Your heaviness flattens you to the earth
Upon rocks thy back will lay uneven
Where is there a library where words
Softly cushion time's mannerisms
I pray that you find doors all open
All guides straight unbroken
Canticles of hymns soft spoken

A highway no need for tokens

Rabbi Schlotz Talks With Satan: Day91

Rabbi:
bells distant span sound stretched
miles of lacerating filters sweep
light house beacons mysterious
as whales heard over tumultuous
cities sounded alarms dying
as bewildered beasts extinct
by echoes spun between planets

our voices plead against walls of vibrations
we beg for mercy not knowing our own sins

we eat the communion wafers of ignorance
watch hands of dead priests raise hosts
with withered skeletal fingers aloft in silence

gone is our hope
no more of brightness
nothing but plodding
of disemboweled featureless famine

before heavens shaken loose of gravity

we, you and I, are the remnants of shale shook loose
from sweated scales of impassable cliffs run smooth

by avalanches overpowering magnificent elbows
of spiked pillars of pointed stone swords piercing air

Satan:
Your writing scares and bores me.

Rabbi:
alight as faceless riders bowing to an audience of witches
calm spirits of misguided saints of salvation having no power
to escape from mesmerizing tin-tapping-tension

Rabbi Schlotz Talks With Satan: Day-92

Rabbi:
Can sorrow be avoided?
Like a severed moon
Divisive, impaired?

I come before a door
To choose what life cannot give me.
The Opus Posthumous in C minor
Makes itself heard on both sides of life.

I am swept into a dustpan of musical notes.
Here is the cup of dreams and
Here is repetition of sweetness.

Give over to emotion.
In the grey shallow night,
Push forward to silence.

We catch our breath

Satan:
Go on.

Rabbi:
Stop and start
Until the oceans join hands.
Until both sides of universal
Rivers become one current.

Rabbi Schlotz Talks With Satan: Day-93

Rabbi:
Cover over my faults,
I am bigger than life.
I am part of a gestalt
Torn loose from strife.

I ride currents aloft
Fire hazards schemes
Pillowed dreams soft
Part of winning teams

Take the rocket up
Past earth's rotation
Fill, fill my cup
Awake to new elation.

Rabbi Schlotz Talks With Satan: Day-94

Rabbi:
I have a focus on food service people.
I have an affinity or empathy toward these people who serve us and our hungers.
In Iliad the book by Homer, eating becomes the interruption to the story of battle. Both sides - Greeks and Trojans - stop the battle to feast and play games together.
Great armies of antiquity were accompanied by cooks and wait people serving them.
In serving as a military soldier, we were always surrounded by the mess hall and cooks.
As a customer in many restaurants where I have lived, I am always partial to food industry people. My thanks to these people is always to tip well and let these people know that I not only depend upon being fed by them but always letting them know my appreciation.
In my current restaurant called the "Flaming Grill", I have begun to be accustomed to the wait people and cooks.
I bought some candy and flowers to let the people share who serve us.
Something happened that makes me sad. The wait person or lady that I brought the flowers to took them home, depriving the rest of the restaurant people of my gift.
The next day, when I realized what the wait person did taking the flowers - vase & all - I went back to the florist and had the flowers and vase made over or replicated.

I took them to the restaurant and the remaining wait people put the flowers atop a shelf where they were admired by customers and wait people together.

Not one of the remaining wait people criticized their compatriot partner. They were kind to this person, who I held in disfavor.

I told the manager of the situation and she put a note in the cash register for the thief to return the vase.

The response was word got back to me that the thief would return the vase soon. But, the thief justified what she did and sending the message back to me that I gave the flowers, just to her.

It remains this way with over a week gone.

My years of life have taught me that incorrect behavior will eventually be balanced out.

That is life: balance. We all hope that our lives will be balanced.

Satan:

Ho, hum.

Rabbi Schlotz Talks With Satan: Day-95

Rabbi:
I pray for some people I meet and may never come into contact with again.

Satan:
Be careful. Some of them may be on my list.

Rabbi:
Then, I pray for them to get out of hell.

For Sophia, who wears her wrist jewelry well in dangling fashion and as accent to her wedding ring, shiny and sparkling. She works to keep her family budget tight, even though all her two children are out of the house. She is a Polish woman with young features and a full bodied look of being well fed and comfortable. I pray that she finds peace working so hard in the restaurant making tips and keeping customers happy.

For Emanuella, tall and stately with long fingers and a face stretched into loveliness. A full thirty of age and with tattoos on the back of her hands flowing onto the fingers and up past the wrists. She is a fair faced lady who walks with the grace of an uprooted tree that remains in place as she moves. Her tattoos are branches and flowers that give her movements the feeling of invisible puppet strings guiding her with magical motion.

For Liza with the short stout features of an iron will. She is considerate as she stares directly into your eyes taking your order. Liza has skin unblemished and seamless. She has the tanned skin of rich creamy texture. She is the prettiest of all the waitress's. She will maintain her youthful features long into her extended years as time passes through her.

Satan:

You do not even know these people. Why are you wasting your prayers on common waitress people? Making judgments you are not qualified to make?

Rabbi:

I pray for who I want.

Satan:

You are boring.

Rabbi:

As boring as you are kind.

Rabbi Schlotz Talks With Satan: Day-96

Rabbi:
You are blue as evening true where butterflies rest
Whispering birds asleep sealing nights star canopy
You are blue as loons leaving their echo across weeds

Do not get carried away by the silence of blue streaks
Across a silver canvas of waiting ghosts half awake
I think of you like embers of a dying fire of volcanoes
I wish for you in myself starting memories of pain
I am misty with bursts of flowers beneath my eyes

And you are as indigo diffused as a symmetry of grey
I miss the light coming through closed window panes
Carrying with it images of your smile composed free
Seems like the oceans are too far to see across
Seems like air of forest breathing into the dark
Cannot be real without you beside me in perfume

I am able to see without eyes
Feel without fingers
Touch you without
You being here

Can my heart be anything
But a reminder of you, blue

Satan:
You have got love, bad.

Rabbi:

Galileo said to the court officials, as he was being taken away to his imprisonment, "It does not matter what you say or think, in the morning the earth will continue to circle the sun."

Neither you nor God are in total control of your powers. It does not matter what you both say, new rules will dispatch you two to posterity of oblivion. The new God and new devil will come from artificial intelligence.

You see, simple expediency is upheld with evolution. When goats deprived turtles of food on Galapagos Islands, the introduction of sugar to the island, took over as the major food for the turtles.

So, the turtles adapted. That is how God and **The Devil** will adapt, from the introduction of mechanical sophistication of the computer and all the evolving choices of software and hardware.

Satan:

You seem confident. But, you seem to forget that God and myself are more aware than you know. We have, long ago, begun our adaption to a new situation. We are steps ahead of changes in belief systems. Religion, in all its forms, has changed to the changing philosophies of humanity. Neither God nor myself will die out. We will adapt nicely, in time.

Rabbi:

Maybe you will adapt, but you will not have the power over people, in time.

Rabbi Schlotz Talks With Satan: Day-98

Rabbi:
I am not sure what her hate is worth.
Does she think that I am going to cave in and kill myself?
Does hate make her feel good?
She sees herself in the mirror and hates what she is?
I will not hate her back in return. It is useless.
I will continue to pray for her before I go to sleep.

Satan:
I can teach you to hate and feel good about it.

Rabbi:
No thanks.

Satan:
Hate; free of guilt.

Rabbi:
Guilt; free of hate.

Satan:
Hate is so easy. You can almost never run out of things to hate.

Rabbi:
Hate costs a lot.
To hate, one has to give up joy.

Satan:

People that hate feel great satisfaction.

Rabbl:

What a shame to hate to feel good.
It is so much easier to love and feel good.

Satan:

Not by my observations.
Once a person is caught up in hate, I can take my eyes off of them.

Rabbi:

Oh, so you watch for hate?   No wonder you love hate. Hate endures you to dark evil.

Satan:

Stop flattering.

Rabbi:

I will make you a deal; I will offer you all the money in the world to give up hate.

Satan:

I already have all the money that exists.   All the people who hate and sign their souls over to me leave their money to me, in a manner of speaking.

Rabbi Schlotz Talks With Satan: Day-99

Rabbi:
I am finishing this series of conversations and related poems called Talks with Satan.
Have I learned anything by these discourses?
Well, I, like most people, hold beliefs that we cherish that stay in place until we are shocked out of them.   Nothing here was a shock. I started out not believing that Satan exists and I still feel that Satan only exists for souls that need him.

Satan:
You need me, if only for opposition to your staunch fears.
Otherwise, I would not be here talking to you.

Rabbi:
It is true I fear. I do not fear eternal damnation. I fear only ignorance. I fear that I may have done something to offend God, Satan or any of my contemporary human beings.
Neither Satan nor God judge me. I only face my fear and judge myself. I am the harshest judge of myself.
Let me tell you my biggest fear: I fear the insanity of not being able to differentiate between reality and fantasy.
We are surrounded by so many forms of reality or points-of-view, that we have a hard time knowing what is the right one.

I know that reality changes over time.
Reality is like the brilliance of a burst of star nova where the eye cannot tell the difference between colors, but is blinded by the fusion, to the point that we can only call the color as, maybe, fire.

In the end we burst apart and flow into the white light of color so stunning that we see past our ocular perceptions and into the soul of God so blinding and soothing that we give ourselves over to the grace within the whiteness that exists past the rainbow explosion.

Satan:
You are too much a poet to even call yourself a human.

Rabbi:
I listen to your words and thank you for observing and commenting. You are **The Devil** and your reality is outside of my belief systems. I am but an instrument of questions and rational thinking.
You are obfuscating or like the permafrost that exists below the snow of understanding. You are the hidden meanings of fear. You are the heaven of souls who have lost their way and need the pain of your punishment to keep them awake.
I may flounder around with trying on this idea or that idea, but, in the end, I find comfort in piecing together things to make me whole.

Satan:
Listen, I have offered you eternal happiness in my kingdom and that offer stands any time you want. I have spent a lot of time trying to convert you and I wave goodbye to you as the seas close over our time.

Rabbi Schlotz Talks With Satan: Day-100

Rabbi:
I call to the flowers of creation to bless my book and poems.
I give over my gratefulness to the sorrow of elapsed time.
My heart is full of time-gone.
Layers of time coil around me to protect my feelings.
Love has been my guide leading me over the cliff of
understanding.

Love has been the cursed-blessing of my salvation.

I often confused love with my search for affection. I get so
mixed up with desire and love. Desire is a one way street to
unhappiness.

Here is my offering to a God who refuses to become visible.
I give my offering over upon the altar of supplication.
Prayer and offering are things we leave below the feet of an
invisible deity. We leave and never look back for fear that we
will turn into a pillar of light and disappear.
Happiness is the ring we toss the ball through. There is an
instant when the net allows us to pass and then life is over.

Come thou mystery of shrouded thoughts.
Come whilst my heart can hear blood.
The blood that gives life and the blood that carries away all pain.
I have no more thoughts but silent acquiescence to forces that
sweep me away into oblivion.

Last but first, somewhere where first shall be last.

Colored into pale indifference.
I exist till a blur of defacement wipes me clean from the universe.

Satan:
Amen.

Author's Biography

Michael G. Thomas is a CPA residing and working in Sterling Heights, Michigan who is best described as a warm and cuddly curmudgeon. He has been writing for decades, primarily poetry and short stories, but has a love of plays and theatre. Mostly, he defies description, not because he is nondescript, but because the proper words have not been invented. Those who know him well will tell you he is well worth knowing, and that is the best biography one can have.

Also by Michael Thomas

ISBN: 978-1500192037

Rabbi Schlotz Talks With God

Michael Thomas

ISBN: 978-1943974726

Rabbi Schlotz Talks to Buddha

Michael Thomas

ISBN: 978-1943974153

The
Plantagenets

Michael Thomas

ISBN: 978-1492297567

Michael Thomas

The Accounting Book

ISBN: 978-1500267889

New Selected Writings

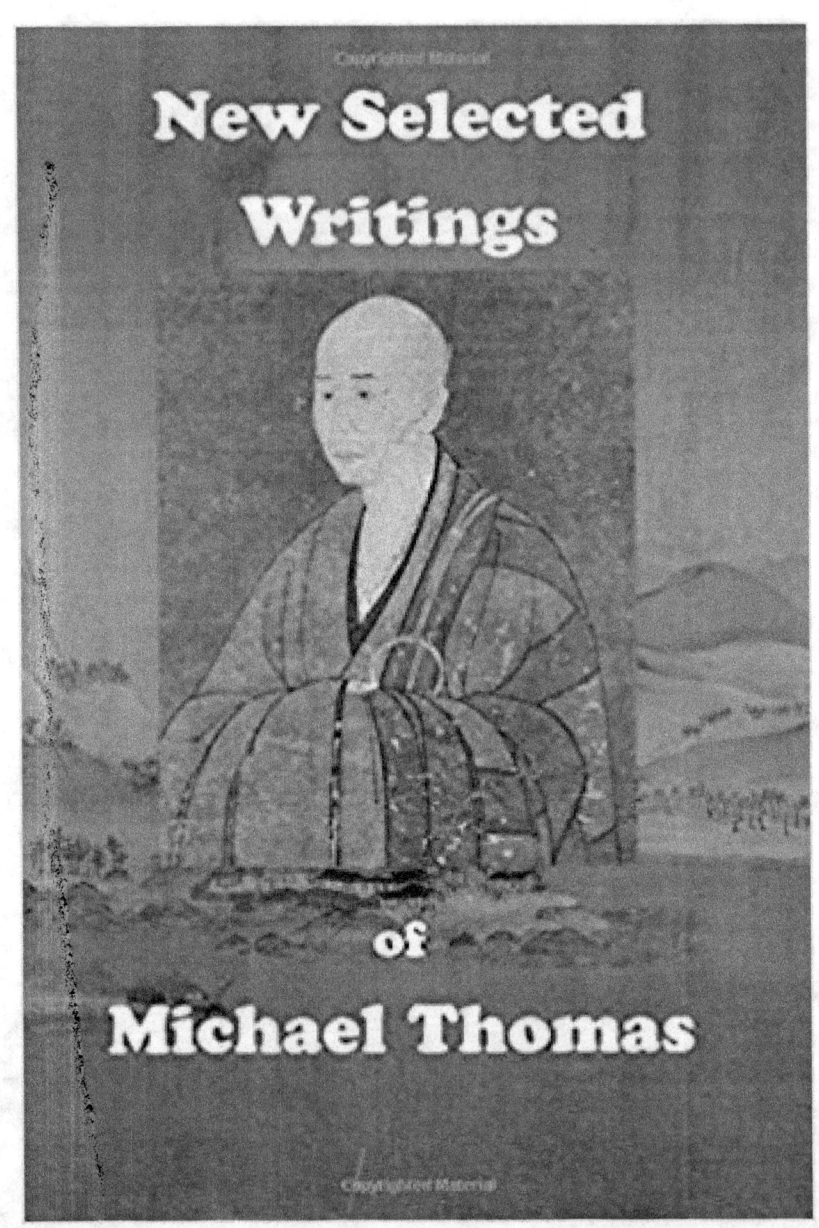

of
Michael Thomas

ISBN-13: 978-1530832071

Michael Thomas Poetry 1

ISBN: 978-1492776932

Michael Thomas Poetry
Volume 2

ISBN: 978-1495419010

Michael Thomas Poetry
Volume 3

ISBN-13: 978-1501063275

Michael Thomas Poetry
Volume 4

ISBN: 978-1507634387

Michael Thomas Poetry
Volume 5

ISBN: 978-1514174104

Michael Thomas Poetry
Volume 6

ISBN-13:978-1523266333

Michael Thomas Poetry
Volume 7

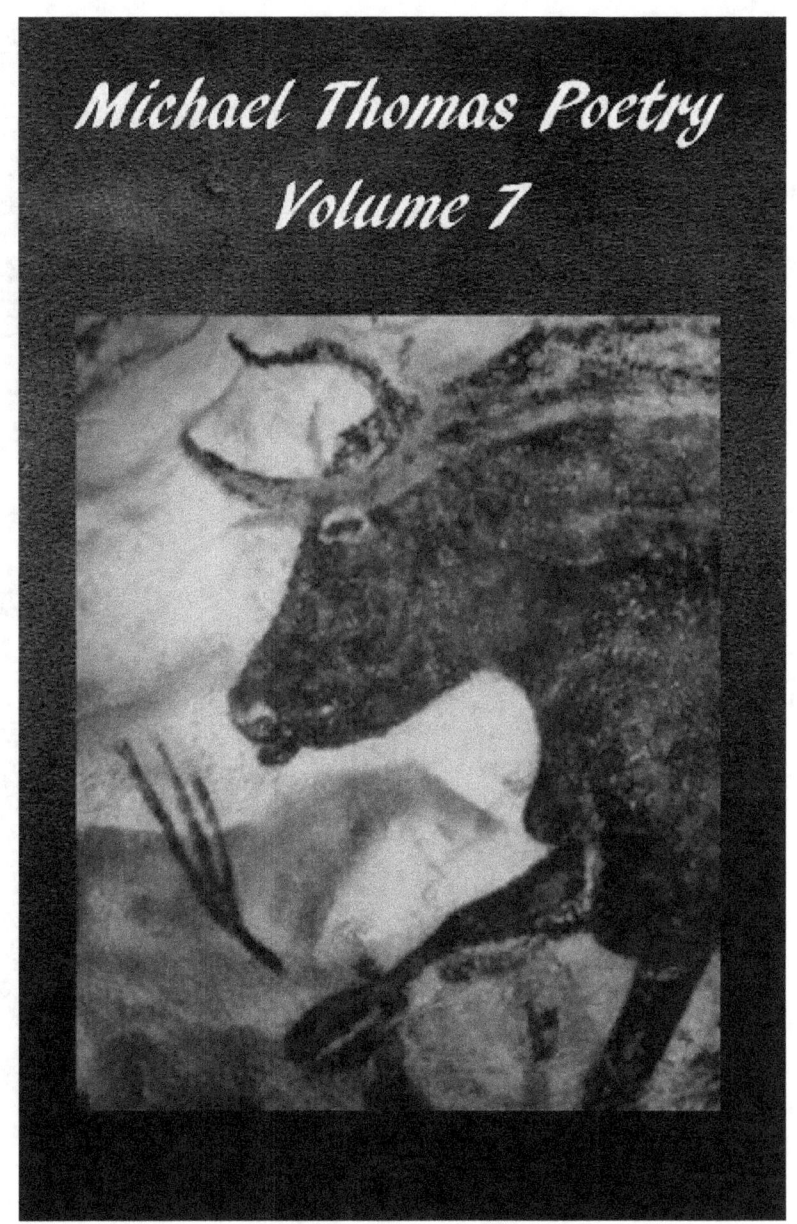

ISBN-13: 978-1-943974-13-9

Michael Thomas Poetry
Volume 8

ISBN: 978-1943974252

Michael Thomas Poetry
Volume 9

These and other books by independent authors
can be found at:

www.shoestringbookpublishing.com

Shoestring Book Publishing offers
simple and affordable quality book publishing.

The _smart_ choice
for the _wise_ independent authors voice!

Send your inquiry today to:
Shoestringpublishing4u@gmail.com
Contact Allan 207-922-8837

Please Review!

All independent authors depend upon reviews left on Amazon.com by readers to help promote their books. Without these reviews, they will hardly get any notice. Please take the time to leave a short review. Simply go to Amazon.com, find the book and go to the book's page. Under the author's name will be a list of reviews and stars. Click here and there will be a big button saying "Create your own review". Please click here and review.

It only takes a minute!